I0788225

I Cum When You Cum

Explicit Erotic Sex Stories MILFs,
BDSM, Threesomes, Anal, Femdom,
Tantric Sex, Wife Swapping, Roleplay,
Forbidden Desires, 69, Orgies
(Orgasmic Collection)

By G.G. Goode

Contents

The Casual Hookup

Lesbian, Femdom, Sex Story

Prostitutes have always intrigued me.

Maybe it was the fact that I was always curious as to why they chose that life, but that's how I ended up at the corner of Westmount and Chestnut, waiting for the mysterious "Ms. V."

Ms. V was advertised as some sort of hot femme fatale, and when I got to her, she looked me over, licking her lips.

"There you are, kitten. I take it you know the password?" she said.

"Spotted duck," I said out loud.

That was the code word that I was given, and Ms. V curled her lips into that of a smile.

"Good girl. So do you have the payment?"

"I do," I told her.

I gave her half of the payment, which was the upfront payment for this kind of thing. Half now and the other half after we're done.

Ms. V was one of the top lesbian femdom prostitutes in the area, and I was told by my friend Whitney that she would be perfect for me. She told me to give a nickname to myself, so Calico it was.

You know, like a cat.

"Very good, Calico. Come with me then. We'll begin," she said.

Suddenly, she moved behind me, grabbing my neck. I thought she would choke me, but a collar fitted nicely there, securing against my neck. The cold leather caused me to shiver.

"Ahh," I said, flushing as she looked at me with her red lips, a smile on her face.

"Does my little Calico like it? You're a good pet," she said to me.

I was a good pet. In fact, I was her pet. And tonight, she'd be all mine.

She put a leash on my neck, securing it right then and there, holding me secure as she walked me over to the hotel, or wherever it was that she did this. She then tugged on it a bit harder, goading me to go as I started to shiver, moaning with delight.

She put a blindfold on to prevent me from seeing where we were going, which was fine.

That's how I assumed this shit was done. We walked, her hand on the leash and the other on my neck, rubbing it slightly.

"Good girl," she said.

Hearing those words, the way that she uttered them, made me melt. I didn't know why, but it just...made me excited, a feeling that I hadn't truly felt in a long ass time.

She then pushed a door open, pressing me down so that I was on my hands and knees, a boot against my back, pressing there.

"Good girl. Now be a good pet and walk down the steps," she said.

So we were going down? I guess I'd do this. She undid the blindfold so that I wouldn't trip and fall, but I did so.

Each pat down the stairs was a little bit harder, simply because I had the leash there, right up next to me, and I shivered.

She then brought me all the way down, pressing me slightly with her boot.

"Good girl. Now get inside," she said.

I crawled on my hands and knees to the room. She closed the door, locking it.

"Good girl. Now down on the bed," she said.

I did as I was told, but then I saw her reach for the collar, taking the leash off, but keeping it on. She then grabbed my hands, pulling them slightly until of course, they were onto each side of the bed, holding me there.

"Ahh," I said to her.

"There we go. You're doing great," she told me.

The positive reassurance combined with her domineering personality made me start to sweat, excitement coursing through my body.

She soon took my knees next, too, pulling them outwards so that my feet were splayed out. I gasped as I felt her restrain my body there, leaving me like a fly in her trap.

She hovered over me, a smile present on her face. It told me everything that I needed to know.

"So my little pet, where would you like me to begin?" she asked me.

Where did I want her to begin? I mean, if she just took me and used me like the little fuck toy I wanted to be, that was fine. But of course, I was paying for her.

I didn't have a ton of time, but I knew that I'd milk this to every level that I could.

"Use me. Make me your pet," I said.

"Well, I'm already doing that. But is there anything you don't want?"

"No...blood or knives or anything that could actually hurt me. And...no scat obviously," I said.

"Alright, pet, well, that leaves us with a lot that we can do. But first, I think making sure that you can't see what's next is probably the best thing for you," she told me.

I shivered, realizing that she meant she'd take my vision away. What would happen next? I gasped as I felt the black blindfold move over my eyes, blinding me from the world around me. My head felt heavy, but the little hands that grazed down my body made me shiver with delight.

She got to my breasts, touching one of the nipples, watching me shiver with delight, moaning in pleasure as she laughed.

"Look at you! So turned on. The desire is obvious," she said.

That much was sure. I knew that she was making me into her little pet, and the only thing I could do was to sit there and take it.

I felt her hand move upwards towards my breasts, touching the very tips of them. Then, I felt two fingers against my nipple, pushing me there, holding me as I could feel her eyes boring into my own, even while blinded.

"So turned on....do you want a mistress to make you feel good? Or do you want a little bit of pain first?" she asked.

"Ahh, pain, please, mistress," I said.

The pain was such a pleasure for me. I was so turned on by the way that she took care of me, making me feel good, and the fact that I could feel her hands slowly skate over to my nipples again, touching them slightly, was enough to turn me on, to make me groan and shiver. She pressed two fingers there, holding the edge of my nipple, and that alone was enough to make me gasp out.

It was heavenly to feel her hands there, touching me, teasing me, and making me lose control. Her touches felt so rough, and when I felt a pair of clasps touch the tip of my breasts, I cried out.

"Quiet there, dearie. You need to be a good pet," she said.

She put the clamps on each of my nipples, but they were different from the ordinary pulling clamps that only involved two sides. No, this involved both sides, and when I felt her tug on this a little bit harder, I started to shiver, crying out, feeling it take hold of me. I grabbed the restraints, holding them there as she teased the tip of my nipple, which had become more sensitive due to the clasps, of course. I was at a loss for words, unsure of what to say, but of course, completely immobilized by the pleasures of the flesh, of the moment, and the ache and desire which flooded through me. I wanted nothing more than to relish in this pleasure, to enjoy everything, and to feel this as well.

She continued teasing me with her fingers, every slight touch dancing over the tip of my nipple and making me shudder and cry out. I was losing it, but I knew that she wouldn't stop at this. She would give me pleasure that I knew I'd remember and love forever. I was the dog, the pet that this mistress had, and I loved everything about it.

The mistress then stopped with the nipple teasing, but that didn't mean she got rid of them. She ended up moving her hands away, and I felt the rummaging of something. When it came back, I felt something soft and teasing right up against the tip of my armpits, tickling there. I started to giggle, squirming about as she continued tickling my armpits.

My armpits and sides were very ticklish, and, usually, I wouldn't say I liked this. But I did specifically ask for this in the planning with the mistress. Maybe it was the fact that she would treat me differently than anyone else. Still, there was a thrill in letting her masochistic tendencies out, teasing me, making me feel pleasure and awe, and enjoying everything she could give me. She soon moved her little feather tickler downwards, but she didn't move past the edge of my armpit. Instead, she teases the very edge of it, causing me to let out a small groan, teasing, feeling the pleasure, and enjoying everything that came out of this.

I felt her do this again, causing me to yelp, but not before moving downwards, moving her hands to one of my sides, lightly grazing her long, red fingernails against there. I wondered how those would feel inside me, and the thought of that made me want to just lose it right then and there.

She moved her hands towards one of the sides while she let the tickler move underneath my breasts, touching them there. I didn't expect such a feather-light sensation against there to make me cry out in pleasure, the feeling of this a massive turn-on for me. She soon moved her hands towards my stomach, teasing the edge of it with those same fingernails as she continued tickling my sides. She started tickling me a little bit harder, and that, of course, caused me to laugh my ass off, holding the restraints and giggling up a storm as she did this. There was a thrill that came from being at the mercy of her, for being turned on by this, and this alone. The way she continued this, the passion and feeling that came over me was enough to drive me to the brink.

After a moment, though, she simply stopped, pulling away for a second.

"What's that, my pet?" she said as she heard me groan.

"It felt...so good," I said. The lack of ability to move made the tickling that much more prominent, and of course, I howled with laughter as I thrust my hips upwards, enjoying the feeling of this. She continued to smile, touching the very tip of my nipple once more, this time with the longest fingernail, grazing the edge of it there.

"Look at you, my little pet. You seem to enjoy the pain somewhat. If I'm hurting you, always say so, but I don't think I'll be doing anything you hate, though," she said.

"Not...at all," I said to her, barely able to make out the words that I wanted to say. It was hard to form coherent sounds when I felt her hands there, completely teasing me, making me shiver with delight, feel turned on, and enjoying all of this too.

She then slowly moved my restraints so that I was around on my tummy now. She leaned her body over mine, her voice right in my ear.

"Look at you pet. You're so turned on. I can't wait to see what you've got in you," she said, letting her tongue snake against my earlobe. The sensation of this sent a chill through my spine, the realization that I was hers, and hers alone, a totally rewarding and amazing experience.

I loved this, and I knew that she enjoyed this too. There was something nice about being taken like this and turned on at the same time. I rarely got to feel this level of pleasure as I started squirming about, enjoying the feeling of it all.

She smiled, chuckling as she did so. I knew that she was happy with the results of this, given how my body reacted, thrusting forward as I let out a small gasp. Her hands then slowly dragged down my back, moving downwards. It was so deep I wondered if she would draw blood.

But she didn't. Instead, she let her hands rest slightly against the very edge of my butt, moving her fingers up and down, slowly creating lines up and down my back. The little touch of it was enough to turn me on, driving me crazy and making me feel the rush of pleasure.

She dug her fingers in, pressing against there, making me suddenly cry out and feel the pleasure surge through my body. She let out a small hum, touching there, listening to the sounds that I uttered.

"There you go....good girl," she cooed in my ear.

She dug her nails a bit further until, of course, she got right towards the edge of my backside, touching there, tickling about. I shivered, crying out loud as I felt the hands just barely graze against me.

It was all so stimulating, so shocking to me, that I couldn't get enough of it. I wanted more, and before I knew it, her hands moved towards my ass, grasping it.

"Good girl. You have a wonderful ass," she said.

"Thank you, mistress. It's all yours," I said out loud.

She let out a small chuckle, and I felt my whole body stay on edge. That's when I felt it.

The smack of her hands, the echo of the feeling as it hit me, and the cry that came out of my mouth. She smacked me hard, hitting me there. I cried out once again after the third one, realizing that her hands were all on me, driving me insane, making me ache for her.

"There you go....I can see that you're slowly coming under my control and being a good little pet," she said.

"Yes, I am," I breathed out.

She smacked me once more, causing a guttural sound to emit from my mouth. The ache, the need, the desire for her, it was all stimulating me in ways I didn't expect to feel. I wanted this, though, and I knew that, with every single touch, it would set me on fire, making me hers.

She then whacked me once more with her hands before moving away. I felt like there was way too long of a pause for me, and I wanted to just....just accept the whole moment. I soon felt her hands move towards my ass, clutching it once more.

"I've got another special surprise for you," she told me.

What in the world was the special surprise, though? I shivered, imagining what it was that she had under all of this and the excitement she had next for me. She stimulated it, making me ache for her. The little touches were driving me insane.

Then, I felt something different against my ass. It was the feeling of stiff leather, touching and kissing right over the very edge of my body. I cried out, suddenly whimpering with delight as she grazed the little leather strip against my ass.

"Does my little pet like a bit of punishment?" she cooed.

"Yes, mistress," I said.

I liked it when she would tease me like this. She let out a small chuckle before she smacked me once more, causing me to react to her touches immediately. She used the leather flogger on me, every single touch of this making me scream out with delight.

She continued to tease me, and with every single touch, every single motion, I felt like I was losing all semblance of control. Something was thrilling about someone doing this to me.
Maybe it's the masochist in me, but I really liked the way that this was happening and how everything was panning out.

She continued this for a bit until I let out a slight choked sound. She then stopped, moving away, looking me up and down with a smile.

"My little pet is alright?" she said.

"Yes, mistress. I love this. I want...I want more," I said to her.

She let out a small chuckle. "Then perhaps I can give you something that...you will surely remember. I'm going to make you squirm, and you have to beg for me to stop it," she said.

The way she said those words and the little smile that she had made me excited, albeit nervous. There was something almost nerve-wracking about all of this, but then, before I knew it, she moved her hands away from my body. I didn't feel any pressure or spankings, which was what made me wonder what was next.

Before I knew it, I felt a finger behind me, teasing my pussy, little circular motions. I let out a little whine, enjoying the feeling of this. But then, before I knew it, she pushed something into me.

It was big, and I let out a small groan as I felt it fill me up. I didn't mind big; it just surprised me, that's all. She then put it all the way in, letting it sit there for a bit.

"There we go," she said.

She turned it on, and soon, the little vibrator came to life. But what I didn't know was that it also had clitoral stimulation.

So not only was my pussy feeling this, but also my most sensitive parts! I clung to the bed, feeling the restraints there hold me entirely as I let out a low groan.

"You good there pet?"

"Yes, mistress. I want more," I told her.

I didn't expect to become this kind of person, but here I was. She let out a little chuckle before pressing the button, and soon, the vibrator roared to life.

I couldn't believe how good this felt. But also how different it was. It stimulated every single fiber of my being, every nerve ending that hit my core. It was hard not to hold back, to not just cum right then and there, especially given how this felt.

But I held back. I knew that if I gave in right away, the mistress wouldn't like it. And sure enough, she hummed in approval.

"You're persistent. I like that in a pet," she said.

"Thank you mistress," I told her.

"Now, let's see if you can handle more," she purred.

She pressed the button even higher, and the vibrator rumbled to life. I soon felt like it hit every part of me, every fiber of my being, and I shivered, crying out loud.

"Holy shit," I told her.

"There we go. Just take it easy. Be relaxed," she said, her voice soothing to me.

I tried just to feel this way, but it felt like the pleasure was hitting every part of me and that I was losing all semblance of control. After a few more moments, she pressed the button once more, and it was all I could do, not just to lose it right then and there, cumming hard against her.

She smiled, taking the vibrator out and sucking on it. I felt my body slowly fall to the ground, trying to give in, but I knew that this wouldn't be it.

"What's the matter, you want more?" she asked.

"Yes," I managed to breathe out.

"Yes, what?"

"Yes...mistress," I told her, struggling to form coherent words as I looked at her. She let out a small chuckle.

"Gosh, you're so easy to tease. You're already such a mess. There is something quite fun about all of this and about seeing you like this," she told me.

I loved it, too, even though I did feel slightly embarrassed by the way things were going. She did move slightly, moving away once more, but then she spread me apart, pressing her tongue towards my entrance, teasing me a little bit around before diving right in.

I suddenly felt the jerking sensation of this, the amazing feeling that came out of it, and in truth, I was in awe at how good this was. She soon began to move her tongue around in circles, touching and teasing before dipping herself into me, touching me deep within. I felt I was slowly crumbling, right then and there. There was something almost stimulating about all of this.

I enjoyed it, and everything about this was just damn perfect. It drove me insane, and there was nothing more that I could do, other than, of course, to only accept the moment, enjoy the feeling, and just feel it all hit every single part of my fiber, my being, and the excitement that came out of this.

I ached for her. I knew that she enjoyed this, as well, given the way that she teased every part of me. As I sat there, feeling her hit every single piece of me, I tensed up, feeling the closeness of my body, and then, as it hit, I screamed out, feeling my back arch and my body suddenly held itself forward. I came hard, feeling my whole body whimper and my juices flow out. She licked me clean, and I laid there, struggling to remember how to think straight. Then, I felt her slap my butt one last time.

"Good pet. But I didn't want you to cum just yet," she said.

"Sorry, mistress, it was just...too damn good," I told her.

"It's alright pet, I'm going to make you feel even better," she said to me.

She moved her body and pushed mine down so that I was facing her once more. She moved the restraints a little bit so that my legs were up, but then I felt her hand lightly skirt against the edge of my pussy, teasing it slightly.

"You're so easy to tease pet. I love doing this," she said.

In a way, I enjoyed it too. But what I didn't see was the strapon that she had.

It was big, bigger than anything I've seen, in my entire life. And she was going to put this inside of me. Then again, I did ask for this. I wanted her to take me, to fuck me so hard I'd forget things, and soon, as she slid on in, I gasped as I fumbled with the restraints, holding her there, watching with widened eyes as I looked at her.

"There we go. Just relax. You'll be feeling pleasure soon," she said.

I already was, but I didn't know how to convey the feelings that I had adequately. I soon felt her push the dildo in further, and then it filled me up completely. I arched my back, letting out a guttural sound as she moved her body, thrusting deep into me, making me enjoy the feeling of this. I cried out, holding onto her as she did this, and every single touch, every single emotion, it was all just so damn perfect.

After a few more moments, she held me there, but then she moved her hands slightly, adjusting so that she could look at me. She soon moved towards me, kissing me passionately. I accepted the kiss, completely enamored by the feeling of her body against my own. And I couldn't get enough of this.

It was like she knew precisely just how to turn me on, and then, moments later, she moved her body slightly, pressing a switch.

That's when I felt it—the roar of the vibrations. The feeling of this just completely overtakes me. I clung to the straps, wishing I could hold her, but I noticed that she was enjoying this too. She pressed the vibration function, holding onto me, and then she cried out.

"There we go, babe," she said.

"Yes," I told her.

I knew that she was just a woman I'd get to experience for one night, but this night was magical. I loved being taken by the older woman. She started to increase her thrusts, pushing all the way inside of me, making me tense up, cry out loud, and ache for her. It was like a dream come true, and it was then when, after a few more thrusts, she moved her hands towards my clit, teasing it as I felt that, along with the vibrations that came from the toy she put inside of me too.

This was heaven, and I knew that it had to be. I was so enthralled by this, amazed by how just it hit all of the right places, that she simply chuckled.

"Very good pet. You're enjoying this, aren't you?" she said.

"Yes mistress! I love this," she told me.

I ached for more, and it was then when, after a few more thrusts, she pushed in, hitting that one spot, and that, combined with the vibrations, the stimulation, and everything in between, was enough for me.

I had the most powerful orgasm of my life. Before this, I always thought that this would be something that I would just accept for the moment, but she simply held me there, causing me to let out a series of small cries, feeling the orgasm as it didn't just hit my pussy, but it seemed to hit every single part of my body, and just made me feel like my core was practically fully stimulated as well.

I loved this, and I knew that she enjoyed this too. It was only then that, after a few mere moments, she slowly moved away from me, looking at my spent body, smiling at me.

"Looks like I was a bit too much for you pet," she said.

"No, you were fucking perfect," I told her.

"Very good. I'm glad that I could be perfect for you and show you an amazing time," she said.
She really did, and it was a feeling that I didn't even expect to understand or to feel. I looked at her, and then she took the restraints off, rubbing a bit of lotion on there to help with the burn from the restraints.

"There we go. How's your butt and body," she said.

"Good. A little sore, but I'll manage," I told her.

She nodded.

"Very well. I'm glad that you're okay, though. So you'll be alright," she said.

"Yeah I will be. And your money is...right there in the pocket of my pants. Take it," I said.
She looked at me with a bit of concern.,

"I'd prefer if my clients paid me. I don't take money without them giving it to me," she said.

I knew that made sense, but that made things so much fucking harder because I felt like I had significant weight on my body. With a sigh, I scrambled over to my feet, heading over to where my pants were, grabbing them and the wallet. I brought the bills out, giving them to her.

"But this is double what I asked for," she said.

"Take it. You deserve it," I said.

She really did. She was such a good call girl. I saw her smile.

"Thank you, pet. Just remember if you ever need someone to take care of you, I'm here for you. And maybe next time I can have it be my treat," she said.

"You don't mean...free do you?" I said.

I didn't want to cheat her out of her money, but she shrugged.

"I'm sure we can arrange something there. Now, let me lead you out of here," she told me.

I wanted to stick around, to get to know her, but I'm sure she probably had other clients—probably some men into being pegged by her, or maybe even more.

I didn't want to think too much about it, but also...I wished that I could stay here with her, for a long time. But I knew for one that it probably was for the best for her just to take care of her job, and work on it.

I'd meet up with her again; I was sure of it.

"Alright, let's make our way out of there," she said to me.

I finished getting dressed, and she goaded me out of the area. I didn't know why, but I felt like I was missing something. When we got to the corner where she met, she took the blindfold off, looking at me with a smile on her face.

"There we go," she said.

"Yeah. That was amazing, by the way. Thank you very much," I told her.

"Yeah, I'm pretty happy with the way things went. Don't worry, I'll be looking for you in the future. And next time...maybe we can go even harder," she said to me.

Even harder? I was surprised that she even had a more complex function. I did enjoy the fact that she wasn't the type to run away from a little bit of pain, though, and I nodded.

"Yeah, I wouldn't mind that," I told her.

She gave me a small kiss on the lips before heading off, walking down the alleyways and suddenly disappearing as she left the area.

I stood there, remembering the lingering soreness that was there and what she did to me. There was something just amazing. I didn't know why, but there was definitely an exciting moment as I thought about this.

I didn't mind the idea of seeing her again. I just was worried it was a bit much. But I knew that finding her was the right thing.

She knew how to make me feel things that I'd never experienced before, and I couldn't help but want more of it. It was weird just how much I wanted it, but also, I couldn't help but also wonder if this unlocked something within me, something new, exciting, and unlike anything I'd ever felt before.

The Hooded Man

Dark Romance, Restraint, BDSM

I didn't know why, but I was suddenly feeling like I was being watched. Maybe I shouldn't have gone to the park at night.

But perhaps that was the thrill. That was what I enjoyed about this. The fact that someone...somewhere could just come out at any time and do this to me was both scary as shit but also thrilling.

I walked through there, stepping into the forest. I was supposed to meet my friend Tanya out here. She told me she had a bag of weed for me with my name on it. And lord knows that I needed something to take the edge off.

And if I couldn't get dick, I guess I'll get the next best thing.

I walked a little bit around, seeing the shadows that were there. It made me nervous but also excited me.

"What if someone was out there, waiting to jump me? Would be scary as shit," I said to myself.

I uttered these words, but I couldn't help but wonder if I really wanted that to happen. I felt excited, but I was also a little bit nervous about what would happen next.

That's when I noticed it. The shadow of a person. Was I losing my mind? Maybe I was, and this was just life's way of telling me.

No....it couldn't be, could it?

That's when I whipped my head around. I heard the creaking of a branch, but when I got there, I didn't see anything. I pursed my lips, the revelation that I was being followed, watched, or something of the other hit me.

"This isn't good," I said to myself.

Though deep down, I kind of wanted something to happen. I didn't know; maybe it was that fucked up part of me that craved something like this. But perhaps it was also the part of me that wondered just what in the world would happen if I was attacked out here.

I kind of wanted this.

I started to move once again, seeing the shadows once more. This shit was eerie. I wanted to know if the rumors of someone living out here were true.

Then, I noticed it. The scurrying once more, the sound of the trees, and then, I noticed something getting closer and closer to me.

"W-whose there?" I asked.

I looked at the guy. He had a hood on so that I couldn't recognize his face. Was he some sort of stranger, or was he a friend? I didn't even know anymore. But I definitely was a little bit worried about what would happen next. I began to move away when I felt the force right behind me, holding their hands there, silencing me.

"Don't make a goddamn sound," he said to me.

I tried to say something, but I didn't want to. I figured that...whatever was about to happen definitely wasn't going to be some simple little thing. It would be something huge.

"O-okay," I said.

The voice let out a chuckle.

"I didn't know you'd be so easy to have here, my dear. You shouldn't be out here like this," the voice said.

"Maybe I want to be," I retorted as he moved his mouth. I licked his hand.

I don't know what came over me or if there was any reason for this. I don't know; maybe it was just the thrill of being taken like this.

"A feisty one, are you? Well, I guess that makes it more fun," he said.

His hands moved towards my hips, upwards. The idea of being fucked by a stranger was thrilling. I know that it's not for everyone, but I wanted this, and I craved the feeling.
And it made me wonder if, deep down, he wanted the same thing.

I heard the sound of shuffling, and soon I was up against the tree. I felt my hands tied there, and the hooded man came over, cupping my chin and looking into my eyes.

"What a cutie. You don't seem to be afraid of me either," he pointed out.

"Why would I be? I'm not going to run away," I said.

Running away was for babies, and I knew that he was not going to make me regret this.

"Very well. I guess I can show you just a peek of who I am," he said.

I was worried about this, and I wondered what the hell I was getting into as I stared into his eyes. He smiled, and for a second, I was transfixed by the way he looked.

He had beautiful blue eyes, soft, pale skin, with no hint of stubble. If this were anyone else, I might be more hesitant, but there was something about this man, the way he looked at me, the smile that came upon his face made me feel excited and craved this much more.

"There we go," he purred into my ear.

"Yes," I said.

"You sure you want this? I can let you go, and we can pretend we've never met," he said to me.

I wanted this. I didn't want to leave. Even though I had no idea what this man had in store for me, or even if Tanya would come over to see me at this point, I felt excited as I looked at this.

"Yes," I said to him, my voice breathy and needy.

His lips curled into that of a smile, and soon, I felt his lips descend upon my own. He kissed me hard, holding me there. The touch of this man completely enveloped my quivering body. I didn't want to leave, even though I had a feeling that this may go differently than I thought.

I noticed his hands start to move around my body, touching me. Being restrained meant that I couldn't touch him back, but giving up that power, that need for control, I ached for this kind of thing, and I knew that he liked this too.

The hooded man was someone I'd never met before. Naturally, some people would probably shrink away at the opportunity for this, but there was something thrilling about a man that I barely knew, who would take me like this and make me feel things that I liked.

Was it wrong? Maybe, but also...I liked it. It helped stimulate something within me that I didn't really know that I needed, a want and desire that grew more and more as the night continued.
His lips were amazing, and I felt like I was just drunk off of this. I wanted him, and I knew that this mysterious man, who was here in the forest with me, would give me just that.

His hands moved about, touching and teasing every part of my body that he could without taking off my clothes. I wondered if anyone would see us. I doubted it.

But then, he pushed his tongue in, which surprised me. Albeit I gratefully accepted it, kissing him back, our tongues intertwined, dancing together, and the pleasure was exciting and fun.
It fulfilled a fantasy of mine. A stranger, someone who could show me some amazing feelings, making me excited and ready for more.

He then moved his lips downwards, touching, teasing, and playing with them. I let out a small gasp, surprised by how amazing it felt. It was like he knew exactly where to touch me, which parts that I loved to have focused on, and I felt like I was relishing in everything that went on. His hands moved up towards my breasts, teasing them slightly, his lips hungrily moving downwards, kissing, nipping, and teasing them.

He bit down on my collarbone, hard enough to make me cry out, leaving a mark but not deep enough to draw blood. I shivered, realizing just how good this felt and how much I enjoyed it. I didn't want any of this to stop; something deep inside me was awakening, a feeling I couldn't get enough of. The desire for him...the desire for more...and the lust that seemed to drive me insane, practically crazy, and the lust that I ached for, on so many different levels.

His touch was like a drug, making me shiver, cry out, and indulge in the feeling of this, no matter what. I suddenly noticed that he had his hands right up against the hem of my shirt, pulling it upwards so that, of course, I was exposed partially. My bra was still on, but his hands moved towards my breasts, touching and squeezing the soft mounds, making me shiver.

"You're so easy to tease. I enjoy this. And nobody will hear your cute little sounds. Besides me," he said.

The way he uttered those words in my ear made me cry out suddenly, pressing upwards, understanding of course, that he was the one in control. He was the man behind it all, and I was just here, at the mercy of his touches, and enjoying the feeling of this every which way.
He then moved his hands to where my nipples were, teasing them through the confines of the bra. I suddenly cried out, realizing I could be as loud as possible. The idea behind that excited me because it's not every day I can make noises like this. Showing how much I genuinely enjoy being teased

like this, my aching desire for him, the need for more driving me forward.

He soon moved his hands towards the bottom of my bra, pulling the cups down so that my large breasts tumbled out. They fell, being held up by the bottom part of the garment, and I shivered, realizing how cold it was out here. My nipples hardened, both from the weather and also because of how stimulating this was.

"Look at you, so turned on," he cooed.

He grabbed my nipples, pinching them, and I moved towards the touch, suddenly feeling the excitement of that and the thrill of the moment. He continued to lightly tap at them, teasing them so that they got harder, and soon, I cried out, the excitement and need growing within me.

He pressed and pulled on my nipples, tugging on them and making me shiver. I arched my body forward, realizing how much-limited motion I had due to my hands being tied up, and he smiled.

"Damn, your large cow tits are already so needy. It's clear you like this. You like being my little cow," he said, teasing them against his fingers. He rubbed his hands in circles, causing me to let out a series of guttural moans and sounds.

"Yes! Make me your little cow," I said.

He let out a chuckle, continuing to tease me, making me utter out the neediest sounds I think have ever come out of my mouth. I ached for this, I needed it, and he seemed to get it.

He understood how much I liked it, and I, for one, couldn't get enough of it. He continued to move his hands there, teasing my nipples until they were unbearably hard, and I felt like I was about to burst at the seams. He then pulled one into his mouth, flicking his tongue over the tip of it, making me shiver with delight, the ache for him growing.

I don't know what it is about this man, but there is just...something so amazing about the way that he touched me. He seemed to know exactly how to turn me on, where to tease me, and to let my body lose all semblance of control.

I knew that he enjoyed this too, and there was something just so utterly thrilling about this. He let out a chuckle as he pulled away with a pop, teasing it with the very tip of his tongue.

"Look at you, taking this like a champ. I'm impressed there, cutie," he said.

"T-thanks," I said.

He then suckled on my other breast, teasing the nipple against his mouth before he moved his other hand towards my lonely nipple, teasing the very tip of it with little touches, pressing there and making me shiver with delight. I loved every moment of this, suddenly feeling like I was losing my mind with everything that was happening, the desire for him growing, and the need for his body making me feel even more in shock and awe.

He then moved his lips downwards, taking it fully into his mouth, flicking his tongue around. I was at the mercy of him. I didn't want him to stop, and I knew that I could feel the desire, the orgasm that I had, bubble deep within me.

I knew that I was close to my limit, and he seemed to get it. Well, at least the first limit that I had.

I knew that I wanted more, and I knew for a fact that this was something that excited me, turned me on, and made me shiver with delight, the desire growing within.

He then moved back, right as I was about to release, and I looked at him with slight annoyance on my face.

"Why did you stop?"

"Because I want to make you cum in other ways," he said.

He slid his hands downwards until he got to the edge of my thick thighs, pressing them apart, letting his hands skirt upwards. The way he said those words, the force that came with the way he uttered it, was enough to drive me utterly mad and made me ache for him.

He soon got between my legs, cupping the heat, and as he did so, he let out a small chuckle.

"So wet already. I can't believe you're such a little slut," he said.

He rubbed my clit, touching against there, and it was all I could do, not just let out small, guttural sounds of desire and need, the pleasure growing within me, making me lose everything. The control that I felt, the need for him that was there, all of it was overwhelming me, making me realize just how much desire I had within.

He moved his hands towards the sides of my panties, sliding them downwards with force. I gasped, surprised by the way that this felt. My naked pussy, along with my bare breasts, made me feel so exposed, despite wearing clothes. He smirked, but not before sliding his fingers between my legs. I started moving apart, realizing just how much I ached for him, and how much I wanted this man to explore me.

He rubbed against the tip, sliding his hands around my slippery folds, letting out small gasps as he teased me. I could see the noticeable bulge in his pants and the fact that he was....well, pretty fucking big for lack of a better word. He then slid his fingers around, touching the very tip of my clit, making me utter out small little gasps and moans of arousal. His hands then slid in, right near the entrance, and I braced myself, the need growing.

I was shocked by how easily he was able to tease me.

It wasn't just a tiny little thing either. He was so skillful, every single touch of this driving me closer and closer to the edge. This stranger knew just how to tease me, and I couldn't help but wonder if he knew me from somewhere.

Or maybe he was an ex. But I didn't have an ex who was...this good at this kind of thing. Usually, they'd just eat me out and call it a day. But not this guy.

No, he seemed to have this determined action in his arsenal, to make me lose it, and as his fingers slowly moved in and out, pumping me, moving the tip of his finger against my clit, rubbing it there, I felt my whole body start to slowly grow needy with pleasure. I could feel my legs buckling, but then, he slid another finger inside me, holding it there, teasing the very tip of this, pushing against that area. Suddenly, I felt two fingers in there, pushing against me, and I cried out, trying to move about, but I squirmed under his touch.

"There you go. Good girl," he said.

I loved the way that this felt. The fact that he did this and I was just accepting of it was so much fun. There was something thrilling about this, something that I so desperately enjoyed, and I wanted to just indulge in this moment, and I wanted to accept this from here on out.

He continued pumping his fingers into me, keeping me there as I continued to moan, holding the tree as he did this. Finally, he pushed there one last time, and I cried out, tensing up once more as I suddenly fell back, relieved and enjoying the orgasm that I just experienced.

But then, he pushed me down so that I was on my hands and knees, still bound to the tree. I looked up at him with curiosity. What was he going to do now? He then slowly undid his pants, and I watched with widened eyes as he slowly undid it, pulling his cock out, stroking it.

"How about this? You want it?" he said.

I wanted it inside of me in another way, but I guess I could take this. I slowly moved my lips forward, taking the tip of his cock into my mouth. I sucked on it slowly, hearing the delicious cries that came out of his mouth as I did this. I continued to suck for a little bit, watching him groan with pleasure as I continued to tease him.

"There we go," he said.

I took him further down against my mouth, feeling it slowly gag my throat. I didn't know why, but there was something nice about this. He reached out, grabbing my head, and soon he pushed me down further, holding me there as I cried out, garbled cries that made me shiver with delight.

He started to force my head further downwards, keeping me there and in place.

I started to feel it move closer and closer to my throat, causing me to gag slightly. He held my head there, continuing to jerk himself there. I felt the cock bulge slightly in my mouth, and I wondered what it would feel like deep inside of me.

He continued this for a little while until, of course, he pulled back, looking at me with a smile on his face.

"Look at you, enjoying all of this. You like it when strange men use you," he said.

"Yes," I spat out. I usually wouldn't be this upfront, but the feeling of this was perfect.

He then picked me up, holding my body like it was nothing right over his cock. I was glad that I was on the pill because it led to encounters like this, making things more fun.

He plunged himself into me, and I cling to him with my legs, feeling him pull my body closer.

"That's right, just lay there and take it," he said.

And take it I would. I enjoyed the feeling of this and how he simply knew just how to make me feel good. He started thrusting in deeper, holding me there, and I let out a series of garbled sounds. Being loud in the forest was a fun adventure because it meant that I could be as loud and as out there as I wanted to and that he would just simply take it all right then and there.

He pushed himself all the way into me, filling up my pussy with his fat cock. He held me there, stroking my hair and touching me slightly as he continued this.

"Such a good girl. Taking my cock like this like the little slut that you are," he said.

"Yes, I am a slut," I said.

I loved everything about this, completely enraptured in the pleasure of this and the moment that he shared with me. He continued this for a long ass time, holding me there for what felt like forever, and I could feel him angling his cock, hitting every part of my pussy. I let out a series of tiny cries, moans of pleasure, and he seemed unable to get enough of this. I was his toy, and he would take care of me.

It was rare for me to fall for someone like this when I barely knew who the fuck they were, but I had it bad for this man. With every thrust, every single touch, I was losing my goddamn mind, enjoying the feeling of this, feeling like I was slowly going mad with pleasure at the touches that he gave to me.

After a few more thrusts, he stopped, pulling out of me. I let out a frustrated groan as he laughed at my needy sounds.

"Look at you. So hot and bothered for this. I didn't know you were such a little slut," he said.

"Yes, I am. I need your fucking cock in me," I said.

"You're like a dog in heat. Maybe I should fuck you like one," he said.

I wanted that, and soon, he untied my hands, flipping me around so that I was facing the tree. He then held my hands there again, tying them the other way. But before I could process everything, I felt his cock fill me up once more.

I let out a small cry, feeling the pleasure of this hit every fiber of my being. He was thick, and his cock hit every fiber of my being, making me shiver with delight, crying out loud, enjoying the touch of his body.

Everything about this just felt so damn right. I loved it, and he pushed my head against the bark as his cock filled me up, thrusting into me like I was a dog in heat.

I let out a series of small cries, enjoying the touch of this, feeling like I was at the mercy of this man's touch, unable to get enough from him.

He continued to hold me there, fucking me deeper and deeper, and I simply enjoyed it, relishing in the feeling of his hands there, just taking me, using me like the little slut that I was, and he soon pushed in harder and harder.

His fingers moved to my clit, touching and teasing, rubbing me with subtle, gentle strokes as he pounded hard. The difference in touches, in pleasure, it was all just so raw, and there was something so thrilling about this. I didn't get it, but I knew that he couldn't get enough of it, and it was then when, after a few more thrusts, he let out a groan, pushing himself deep into me, filling me up with his seed completely.

I suddenly felt a hand press against the nub of my clit, teasing me there, tugging on my breasts hard, and as he did this, I suddenly arched my back upwards, crying out loud with a pleasure that I didn't expect, but there was something amazing about all of this.

He soon finished up, pulling out of me as I felt the trail of cum moving down my leg and the shivering sensation of this. I fell to the ground, completely enthralled and lost in the feeling of pleasure that came from this.

As I felt my hands get untied, I moved my body around, looking to see the hooded man there. But there was something different about him. Usually, after getting fucked in the woods by a stranger, normally you'd' feel the urge to run away, right?

Except I didn't want to.

I stared at this person, realizing something oddly familiar about them, but I couldn't pinpoint what that might be.

"You okay?" the voice said.
"Yeah. I'm good. Thank you," I said.

"You're very welcome. You're fun to mess around with," he said.

Something was interesting about his voice. I didn't know what it was. As he walked away, though, I suddenly spoke.

"Wait."

He whipped his head around, looking at me.

"Just who are you?" I asked him.

He simply chuckled, pulling the hood off his face. Who I saw was someone I didn't expect. My boss Lance. He simply smiled.

"Someone you very much know. But you never saw me here. It's best if I be going," he told me.

"Wait, don't go!" I said to Lance.

But before I could say another word, he was gone.

Weirdly, it was Lance of all people. Did this mean something more? Or did he just like to fuck random women in the forest because why not? It was all...so bizarre, that's for sure. And as I stood there, my pants and underwear still in the corner, and my top asunder too in the dark forest, I realized I was supposed to meet Tanya, and that was that.

But I guess I'd meet her eventually, right?

I got myself dressed, still trying to understand why in the world he came out here.

Lance was....well, he was one of the most prominent Executives at the company, and he was also someone who supposedly was dating this really hot woman. So why did he come to the forest and then do this? I didn't get it, and it seemed to make absolutely no sense.

I definitely wondered what would happen now, or even what would come of all of us, because of our encounter. It all seemed so different and not what I was expecting.

I did finally get dressed, looking around, finally figuring out where the pathway was, and then making my way over to where I was supposed to meet Tanya. Did I tell her about Lance, though? I didn't think that was the kind of conversation she wanted to have, of course.

Maybe it was my own personal worries about this, but I also was curious about what may happen now or even what may transpire because of this.

Well, I guess the only thing that I could do at this point was to just wait and see, and maybe, just maybe, Lance will say something.

I got to where Tanya wanted to meet up, and she was sitting there. But I saw the look of confusion on her face.

"Why did you come that way?" she asked.

Shit, I should've gone another way. She probably thinks it's weird that I came from within the forest rather than the parking lot like an average person.

"Sorry, you got here later than I thought, and I was early, so I took a little bit of a walk," I told her.

"Be careful. There are supposedly reports of a creepy ass person out there. They stalk women and will go after them when they are least expecting it," she said.

Was that supposed to be Lance? Did he do this to others? Well, I liked it. It finally fulfilled that role of being fucked in the forest by a random stranger, something that I so desperately desired.

"Well, I'm fine. I'm alive, aren't I?" I said.

"Are you sure you're okay? You seem off," she said.

"Yeah, I'm good," I told her.

We hung out, and Tanya showed me a few things, but they weren't really around here. She was too spooked to stick around this area.

And in a way, I didn't necessarily blame her.

I went back home; there was definitely a feeling of excitement and the desire for more.
I wondered what Lance was doing or if I should talk to him about this. I didn't really have evidence, so maybe he'd forget and just play it off.

Which would suck total ass, but I guess it is what it is, of course.

I wondered though, what would come about with this all. What does one do now after all of this was said and done. He did fulfill a fantasy of mine, and there was something nice about this, but I didn't know what to do next.
The Monday after, I went to work like it was nothing. I saw Lance there, but he didn't make a move or even acknowledge my existence. It was like nothing had happened.

But then, on lunch break, as I sat in the breakroom, I heard the door open. I turned, and there was Lance. There was tension there, making me wonder what he would do now.

"Lance," I said.

"Here. If you want to see me again, you know where to find me," he said.

He calmly gave me a card, showing me the times he'd be out there, in the forest.
"But what about...that girl you're seeing?" I asked.

I felt terrible that I was making him cheat on her, but his lips curled into that of a smile.

"Let's just say that won't be a very long-term affair," he said.

I looked at him, unsure of what he meant; he simply left the card, closed the door, and left.

He didn't say a word to me after that. But I didn't know what it meant. Did things with that new girl go downhill? Possibly, but the idea of this, the way that things were...it was just so shocking that I couldn't believe that this was happening.

And that, of course, also made me wonder what would come about next. What did he have planned for me? Would we just meet up like this? Or would there be more of a plan to it?

There was so much I didn't know, so much that seemed to be hidden away, obscured by the way things were. And of course, I enjoyed this too. It was the beginning of something. A secret kept between the two of us, never to see the light of day, and something that could change my life forever! If things end up panning out in certain ways. My mind goes wild with the thought of it all.

Of course, I'd just have to wait and see.

Miss Layla's Little Maid
Femdom, MILFs

"Hello there, Miss Layla," I said as I walked in.

Miss Layla, the mistress of this mansion and my boss, gave me a small little smile.

"Hello there, Freya. You're early, and you wore the dress too. Great job," she told me with a smile.

I flushed, realizing that this was happening like this. I realized that Miss Layla was always such a damn tease. Then again, I didn't mind it.

In truth, this was probably the best boss that I ever had. She was the one who helped me get the hell out of debt, for starters. When I was desperate and needed a job, I found the ad online, and I decided to scour it. I looked it over, realizing that she needed a full-time maid. So I signed the fucked up.

But what I didn't know was that she wanted...that kind of maid. Not just one to clean her house, but one that was a tease.

When I first joined on, I thought that this wouldn't work out, but Miss Layla definitely showed me that this could be fun. She put me in this tiny ass maid dress, had me clean floors while her hands would move against my body, touching my big butt and cupping it sometimes along the way. I would always gasp and be surprised, but also....I really liked it.

For starters, Miss Layla was older, but there was something about her that made me excited. I didn't know what it was. Maybe it was how she treated me, almost like her little pet, and how she always praised me.

I got off to that. I would be lying if I said that I didn't sometimes head to the bathroom, rub one out, and then go back to see her. She was incredibly attractive. Tall, with long brown hair, big green eyes, and a curvy body. She knew just how to make me a mess, and she was such a tease, which drove me crazy.

But what kind of sucks is that she never went further than that. She would just touch and tease and sometimes get close, almost like she was giving me a kiss. But she never did.

It was so damn frustrating that sometimes I just wanted to scream to her that I wanted her to fuck me already, to pin me down and use me like the little slut that I was. But I never dared tell her this because I feared what may happen.

She might fire me. Perhaps she liked the teasing, and this was her kind of thing. I didn't understand women, but maybe that's all it was.

No....I had a feeling there was something else here, something much, much more.

That day, when I walked in, I saw a look on her face, that of curiosity, like she wanted to say something.

"You alright there, Mistress?" I asked.

"Oh yes, thank you, Freya. Say, are you busy tonight? Do you have to head home early?" she asked me.

Sometimes I'd have to head home to take care of my family, but tonight they'd be fine.

"I don't have to. Why?"

"Because I'd like for you to meet in the master bedroom after your tasks," she said.
Was she...implying something else? I didn't even know, but I couldn't help but feel an excitement course through my body, making me ache for more.

I was worried about bothering her, though, or that I was getting too excited for something that wouldn't happen. She wouldn't choose me...would she?

No, I couldn't think that. That's way too damn good to be true. But the idea of Miss Layla....doing that to me was exciting, and it made me ache for her. It would be a dream come true.

But I didn't want to get my hopes up. However, I did do my work, cleaning up the front room and the kitchen. However, I'd notice her looking over my body, a small smile on her face. It was like she....she had plans, and the way her gaze just penetrated deep into me made me want her, need her, and I craved for her.

But I didn't want to move too fast. I decided the next best thing for me to do would be to wait and see and to hope for the best.

At the end of the day, I went up to the master bedroom. I noticed that the door was slightly ajar. Was Miss Layla in there? I started to wonder about these things, and as I opened the door, I saw her there.

But instead of her normal business attire, she was in lingerie. My eyes stayed focused on her, lingering against her body, and she smiled.

"There you are, Freya. You made it," she said.

"Miss Layla, what is this?" I asked her.

"Simple. I have a special...offer for you if that's what you'd like," she said to me.

"Alright," I told her. I felt my body grow excited as I looked into her eyes. She then beckoned me closer, holding my chin up, staring into my eyes.

"I've seen you," she said out loud.

"W-what do you mean?" I asked with a bit of a flush on my face.

"The way you look at me. You've wanted this, haven't you? For me to just...take you and use you in the ways that I know how to. That's what you desire, correct?" she purred into my ear.

I shuddered, realizing just how much I needed this. I felt my pussy start to moisten at the sound of her.

"Yes," I squeaked out.

"What was that kitten?" she asked.

"Yes. I want this Miss Layla," she said.

"Good girl. That's what I like to hear," she said.

She grabbed my head, pulling it upwards so that we locked eyes. The way she stared at me was just...so lovely. She seemed determined to make me feel good, and I felt so exposed here in this maid dress that I adored it. She pushed her lips to my own, and for a second, we simply kissed.

We stayed like this for a long ass time, both of us enjoying the touch and taste of one another. She was so soft, but also her kiss was forceful like she knew exactly how to make me slowly lose control, the ache and need driving me crazy, and I enjoyed everything about it.

She seemed to get it too, and that's what I liked about it. I felt...happy that she wanted this as much as I did and that there was clearly a need, a desire for her, and a raw emotion that only seemed to grow over time as we kissed then.

She pushed me down on the bed, her lips taking over my own. I was shocked by just how dominant she was, her hands moving against my body.

"You're fine with me taking control, right, Freya?" she asked.

"Yes, Miss Layla," I breathed out. Though deep down, I was about to lose it if she didn't. She let out a small chuckle, pressing her lips harder to me, dominating me.

I'd never been taken by a woman like this, and there was something so foreign about it, but at the same time, so damn perfect, that's for sure. We made out for a little bit, feeling her hips move closer to my own and the touch of her hands sending sparks through my body.

I gasped, feeling her touch and grab my sides, teasing me there. Just that touch alone was enough to drive me crazy, and feeling her hands there was enough for me.

"Good girl. You're already so eager and needy. Let me guess you've wanted this?" she asked.

"Yes," I breathed out finally, after remembering how to use words. I'd be lying if I didn't.

"Really now? Tell me how much you've wanted this," she said to me.

"I mean....I really wanted this a lot. I wanted...you for a while," I said.

"Tell me how much, though? Come on, don't be shy," she said.

Should I really tell her...that? Well, she seemed determined and eager to get an answer out of me, so I sighed.

"I really want you. I've thought about it and.... it's something I've desired for a long ass time," I told her.

"I see. Well, to tell you the truth, I've wanted this too. I just wasn't sure if you wanted it. But I guess since you said yes...I can make you feel things you've never experienced before. Especially with a woman," she said.

Just hearing those words was enough for me to lose all semblance of control, feel turned on, and enjoy the moment at hand.

I felt excited just kissing her, and it brought forth feelings that I couldn't get enough of. Her lips were so amazing, driving me crazy, and I ached for more from this. She soon pressed her body against my own, touching me slightly, and it was enough to make me lose control but just for a moment. I knew that she liked this as much as I did, and I frankly enjoyed the hell out of it so far.

Her lips began to trail downwards, touching the tip of my neck, enjoying the little sounds and moans that came out of there. She let little touches and brushes move downwards, until of course, she got to my collarbone, teasing and sucking on the flesh there. I shivered, excited by the way she moved her lips so skillfully. She then let her hands move upwards, dancing against my neck.

"Just look at you. So turned on. You have such a beautiful body," she said to me.

I cried out, enjoying the sensation of this, and I craved more from her. She then moved her lips towards the tip of my collarbone, sucking on the flesh there. As she did this, I let out a small cry, surprised by how good this felt and the need that came out of my mouth.

I could tell she enjoyed this as much as I did, letting her lips slowly trail towards the very top of my collar, and then, of course, her hands moving towards my maid dress.

"I love this little outfit for a variety of reasons," she said.

"W-what do you mean?" I asked.

"Because I can do this," she said.

She slowly undid the strings on the bodice of the dress, pulling it downwards, revealing my breasts. I didn't have nearly as much as she did, but when her eyes glazed over mine, I saw the haughty look there.

"Wow, very nice, my dear," she said.

I shivered, and then, of course, her hands moved towards my breasts, cupping the area there, touching them slightly. I let out a small cry of surprise, unsure of what to say to her, other than I enjoyed this. She moved her lips towards the tip of one of the nipples, touching it slightly, sucking on the flesh there, making me tense up, cry out, and feel turned on by the sensation of this. She continued to suckle on my breast, causing me to suddenly grab the sides of the bed, holding the covers there and crying out loud, in pleasure, and with an ache that was obvious. She smiled, looking into my eyes.

"Very good girl," she told me.

I cried out, surprised by how just the tiniest of touches was enough to make me like this. I knew that I was excited, but even I was surprised by the way this felt. She soon teased my body, pinching my nipples and moving her lips towards my other nipple, sucking on the flesh there. The touch alone was enough to drive me crazy, making me cry out with surprise, pleasure, and so much more.

I knew that she enjoyed this. There was some sort of thrill she got from teasing me to the point where I was a helpless mess on the bed. Her hands moved up to the tip of my nipple, rubbing there, and then her tongue moved around the sides and then the tip. She looked at me, the apparent need and excitement there, and I shivered. I could see the need in her eyes and just the way...she knew precisely how to make me feel like this. It was like she had this idea all along, and I was hers for the taking.

And yet, there was something nice about that. To be taken by her, worshipped by her hands and mouth, to cum by her touches...this was like a dream come true.

I never thought that I'd dominate her at all. I always felt that she'd be the one to exercise control and to make me become this aching, needy mess for her. And yet, I liked that.
The idea of that was a bit nerve-wracking to me, but I didn't mind it in the least.

She soon moved her lips towards the other nipple, letting her tongue circle and tease the very edge before flicking over, and the other hand moved and rubbed with her palm against my other nipple. I let out a small gasp, surprised by this.

"Good girl," she said.
She moved back, and I soon reached forward, grabbing her breasts, teasing and massaging them through the confines of her outfit. She looked at me with abject surprise, shocked by the way that I moved towards her immediately.

"What's this?" she said.

"I want...to make you feel good too," I said.

The truth was, I was so new to this whole thing. She was my first, and I felt slightly embarrassed by that, but I had a feeling that she would definitely be a fun first that I could enjoy.

She pursed her lips and chuckled.

"Very well, my dear," she said.

I moved towards the back of her lingerie, pulling off her bra and letting it fall to the sides. I quickly moved my lips towards the tip of one of the nipples, awkwardly moving my lips there. She chuckled as she saw the awkward struggle that I had.

"You're adorable but so damn inexperienced," she said to me.

"It's not like I have all that much experience, to begin with," I said, moving my tongue and flicking it in the same manner she did to me. Her breasts were so much bigger, and it felt nice just...being taken like this and being able to reciprocate everything. I watched as she smiled, touching my hips as I licked and teased her nipples.

"You don't have to do all of this, though. Tonight I wanted to make it about you," she purred.
I shook my head.

"Maybe I want to," I told her.

I licked and teased her, exploring her breasts, letting my other hand move upwards. I touched against the very tip of her nipple, causing her to let out a small cry of surprise, and then, of course, I did what she did to me before, which was, of course, pinching and then rubbing my palm against the tip of her other nipple.

I noticed Miss Layla's composure start to crumble slightly. Perhaps she intended only to dominate, but I wanted to make her feel good too.

After a little bit, she pushed me back down on the bed, hiking up my skirt, her hands moving towards my thighs, touching them.

"You have the most divine thighs," she purred.

"Thank you," I said, shocked by the way her hands seemed to know exactly where to go. I felt slightly embarrassed by the way she looked at me, enjoying the way that her hands seemed to know exactly where to explore. I wanted her though, I craved her, and I knew that this was something she desired too.

She quickly moved her hands over towards the very edge of my inner thigh, touching the tip of it, moving her hands in a massaging manner towards my inner thigh. She was so dangerously close to my pussy, and in truth, I'd been wet since the moment she mentioned it. The sparks were there, flying, of course, and that made everything even better for me as well.

For a little bit, she simply touched and grazed over the edge of my pussy, causing me to let out a small cry of need, the ache of desire, and everything that seemed to fall through, making me excited for this. She soon moved her hands towards my clit, touching the very tip of it, rubbing there, and as she did so, I cried out, rubbing myself against her fingers.

"Look at you, slowly losing all semblance of control," she said.

"Yes," I said.

I'd be lying if I said I didn't want this, though. She knew just how to touch me, to make me feel amazing, and that, of course, made everything all the better as well. It was like I was experiencing the best thing ever, and she knew exactly how to touch me, to tease me, and to make me feel good.

After a little bit, she soon moved her fingers away, and soon, she pulled off my panties, revealing my shaven, aching pussy. I was dripping, the need increasing, and as she explored my insides, I let out a guttural sound.

"Needy already?"

"Yes," I muttered, still trying to keep myself together throughout all of this.

She let out a small chuckle, moving her hands there, touching the very edge of my clit, moving her fingers about, making me shiver with delight and cry out with pleasure. She soon dipped a finger against my entrance, and I tensed.

"First time?" she asked.

"Yes," I breathed out. I hoped that it wouldn't be too weird for her if she heard that.
But instead, she chuckled, a cute little sound that echoed through the room.

"How cute. It's been such a long time since I've had a first, but I'm excited for this," she said.
She moved a finger towards my entrance, sliding it in. At first, it felt a little bit full, but as she moved her digit around, I let out a small cry, holding onto her as she continued to move and tease. She pushed a second digit into the, making me shiver with delight, surprised by just...how good this felt.

She knew exactly how to turn me on, her dominating fingers making me become a puddle of goo in front of her. There was something just so nice about this, so damn thrilling, and I wanted her so damn badly.

She moved her fingers in and out, an undulating feeling, and as she did this, she pushed her tongue outwards, touching the very tip of my clit, flicking her tongue there, resting it, and moving it around. To the point where I suddenly felt a rush of pleasure as I felt the teasing grow even more so.

"Holy fuck," I said out loud, arching my back and moaning with delight as she continued the actions against me. Everything about this was such a damn turn-on that I didn't know what else I could do besides take this and roll with it.

She continued the motions for a bit, watching my eyes widen and my hips thrust upwards. She then hit against a spot that made me scream out, suddenly surprised by how turned on I felt, and then I felt my orgasm just hit me square in the face.

It was different than it was with myself. This felt far more powerful like she was a pro at this kind of thing. She continued to jerk her fingers, teasing them, and then moving away, looking at me with a smile.

"There you are. Good girl," she said.

I relished in those words, surprised by how much I desired this. She seemed to know exactly how to make me feel good and turned on by the sensation of this. She then moved her hands towards my clit, rubbing it once more and looking me in the eyes.

I was curious, but then she spoke.

"How about we try to 69?" she offered.

I mean, that could work...right? I'd never tried this before, so I was a bit nervous, but I certainly wasn't going to be against it in the least. I suddenly felt her body get over me, her wet, pink pussy there for me to see.

I tried to do like she did, shoving my tongue into there, exploring and teasing her body. As she did that, she spread me apart, her tongue diving in, exploring me.

I let out a muffled scream, surprised by this but more shocked at the sounds that I made her feel. She seemed to be enjoying this too, and I could tell from the little cries and such alone that she was getting into this. But then she pushed her tongue in deeper, pressing against that one spot, and when she did, I suddenly felt like time had stopped, and I tensed up.

I didn't want to cum yet. I wanted to make her feel amazing, and I wanted to see her lose control, creating a whole different person. But I knew that she wouldn't give in. I was so close, and with every single touch, every single movement of her fingers, the way she pushed her tongue and fingers into me was more than enough. I was drunk off the feeling of pleasure, completely amazed by how amazing this was, and then, shortly after, everything went white. I cried out, arching my back as I came once more. She then let out a small moan, moving herself off of me. I wanted to bring her to orgasm, but then, she looked at me, a needy smile on her face.

"How are you holding up?" she asked me.

"Pretty...good actually," I told her.

"Very good. I guess I can ask if you want more. I have a special toy that I'm sure you'd love," she offered to me.

I realized what she meant by that. She wanted to top me, and she knew how to use a strap. I shivered, nodding.

"Please," I said.

It was weird to desire a woman so much. In the past, I had little crushes and the like, but they never amounted to…wanting someone so damn badly. She then gave me a small little grin, touching my hips, rubbing them there.

"I promise I'll be nice and slow. I can show you what real pleasure is," she said.

The way the words came off of her mouth made me suddenly feel heady. I wanted her to just take me and make me feel things that I otherwise wouldn't get to feel. She was so experienced, and I felt like this was one of the best moments of my life.

I quickly nodded, watching as she moved towards the drawer that was there. She got a strapon out, but it was double-ended. She grabbed some lube, shoving it into herself slowly, letting out a small gasp. When she was done, she spread me apart, looking me in the eyes.

"Everything okay?" she asked me.

I nodded, feeling her eyes glaze over my body, the need in her eyes obvious.

"Yes," I told her.

She beamed, sliding herself slowly into me.

This was different from just fingers, and when she fully breached me, I let out a small, guttural sound. She looked at me with slight concern on her face.

"I'm not hurting you, right?" she asked.

"No, it's just...different. That's all," I told her.

I'd be lying if I said this was a familiar sensation. It was not, but that didn't mean I disliked it in the least. Instead, I enjoyed the hell out of it. The fullness of my pussy with how she looked at me, I could just imagine this moment forever in my mind, and I'd love and cherish it forever.
There was always something truly exciting about this and something that I liked. She slowly began to move her hips a little bit into me, and as she did that, she looked me in the eyes, a smile on her face.

"Are you good?" she asked me.

I nodded, unable to perform words or sounds other than that of lust, desire, and pleasure. It was so obvious that she was enjoying this too, and of course, I was completely enamored by everything that she did to me that it was only a matter of time before she took this further.

And further, she did. She grabbed my legs, pulling them to her shoulders, bending them down. She then moved deep within once more, and then, shortly afterwards I let out a small cry, holding onto her as she pounded into me. She continued this, causing my eyes to widen in shock and surprise, and it was then when, after a few more thrusts, I felt something against my clit.

It was her finger, and I was utterly amazed by how good this was. But then, moments later, I moved my hands upwards, touching her clit too, rubbing it at the same time. She then looked at me with slight surprise, and I smiled.

"I want to make you feel good, too, mistress," I said.

And that was that. She pushed her finger into a certain position, hitting that one part inside of me, and as she did that, I rubbed her again too.

After a few more moments, the two of us looked into one another's eyes, crying out each other's names as we sat there, embracing one another as we felt the high of our orgasms and then slowly coming down, of course, of everything else.

I felt amazing after all of that, and when I came down from that high, I noticed that Miss Layla had pulled out, putting the toy away, and laying down on the bed next to me.

What do you do at this point? Do you…talk about it? I'm not really that good with this kind of thing, but when I looked into her eyes, I saw a slight smile.

"You did well," she said.

"Thank you. That was...amazing," I said. That really was the best way to describe it. I felt like I just got a chance to experience something novel, something amazing, and I loved every goddamn minute of it.

But what do you do next? What now? I kind of was curious. I looked at her, and she took a deep breath.

"You know, there's a lot that we can say here, and a lot of things that well...we could discuss, but I guess the best thing to say is that I had a wonderful time. And I knew that you wanted this for a little while. So I'm glad that I can make you feel good," she said.

I flushed crimson, nodding.

"Thank you. The same to you," I told her.

"With that being said, we have to keep this under wraps. I don't want anyone to find out about this. Not even those who are close to me. If the press discovered this...it wouldn't be good," she said.

That's right. Miss Layla was one of the strongest businesswomen in the world. If people found out about this, it would be a bit of a scandal, to say the least.

"Yeah, I get that," I told her.

"Anyway, I want to see you again Freya. You're such a good maid, and I wouldn't mind if you...stuck around a little bit. I enjoyed this, and I know that you seemed to like this too," she purred in my ear.

"Yeah, I did," I said.

I didn't know if this meant that she was going to hook up with me or not, but I liked the way that this sounded. She leaned in, giving me a kiss on the lips, and I kissed her back, enjoying this.

There was something special about kissing a woman like this, and there was something I so desperately enjoyed.

She then pulled away, looking into my eyes.

"Don't worry, you'll also be getting a nice little bonus from me for this," she said to me.
I flushed. A bonus sounded heavenly.

"Thank you," I said.

"You're very welcome. I'm really excited for you," she said to me.

I felt happy about this. I mean, there was something about the way that Miss Layla treated me that told me I was making the right decision, especially involving her. It was rare for me to feel this good about something, but knowing that I gave such a beautiful woman my virginity and also getting to experience a whole new world with her was just....I couldn't get enough of this.
I did put my clothes back on, but as I was about to leave, I felt her hand against my backside, cupping my ass. She touched me there, and I shivered.

"I can't wait to have you again," she purred.

"I can't wait too, Miss Layla," I said.

And I meant that. I didn't want to lose this chance. I walked on out of there, knowing that this sealed my fate and the future that I'd get to have.

I was excited, to say the least. I didn't know why, but the fact that she could make me feel these things was such a damn thrill. I was excited for more, excited to experience all of this, and I knew that she liked this too.

What did this mean for me, though? I honestly didn't know, but I was just about ready to relax and wait to see what the future has in store for me, both with this job and, of course, with Miss Layla too, and the future she wanted to bring to us as well. I figured it was the start of something new, something amazing, and I was already excited for what it brought.

College Witches

Orgies, Lesbian

I never believed in the paranormal.

At least…that's what I told myself.

I'd always say that it was some bullshit, some crap used to lure stupid women in. That is, until I met Aya.

Aya was…something else, that's for sure.

It all started when we were in class together. The professor told me that we'd be working on a group project. Naturally, I expected it to be some sort of stupid project that we'd have to word ourselves to work together.

But Aya was different. We clicked right away.

Almost too well if I do say so myself. She was super chill, very cute, and honestly….I couldn't get enough of her. At first, it was just a little bit of studying, and some playful flirting. But I always got the feeling that there was much more there, and that she wanted to say something else, but she never did.

That is until about a month after we started the project.

We went over to her dorm for the first time. She seemed nervous, but when I walked in, seeing all of the different spell books and interesting content in there, I was floored.

"Wow, this is all yours?" I asked her.

She nodded.

"Yeah, I'm curious about the occult. I've started talking to other girls who aren't in it, and I figured that maybe...it could be good for both of us," she offered.

She did say that before but I also felt like...it may not be the right thing to do.

"What do you do in those meetings? If you don't mind me asking," I said to her.

She turned to me, a small smile on her face.

"If you want, I can show you," she said.

Wait, she was getting me in the occult? I don't know if this was a good idea or a terrible one, but Aya was hot, and she was kind of weird, so maybe things would work out. She told me that the next meeting of course would be during the full moon.

I probably should've been more careful. I mean, isn't this how girls get sacrificed to Satan or other crap, was it? Maybe, I'm not totally sure. But I followed Aya over to a small, abandoned building that was on the edge of town. When we got there, she said some words, and with a flash, the door opened.

"Come on in," she told me.

I didn't know why, but the idea of this felt a bit nerve-wracking so to speak. I felt a bit scared, and I had no clue what would happen next. I walked on in, and there was a coven of four other girls.

"Hello ladies," she said.

"Hello Aya," the girl on the right said.

"That's Rachel. The one next to her is Elaine. The bigger girl is Shana, and the other one is Monica," she said.

I waved to all of them, and they all scoured me over, like they were looking for something.

"So you're the newbie, aren't you," she said.

"Yeah. This is...interesting," I said.

"You'll have fun," Rachel said.

I noticed Shana looking me over the longest, and Monica giving me a wry smile. Just what the hell were these ladies up to?

I had no clue, and I could feel the slight nervousness that flooded through my body as I thought about this. There was something about this which felt so damn off-putting, that I couldn't really pinpoint why I feel this way.

But, it's not like there was much that I could do. I plopped down at the chair that was empty next to Aya.

They began by saying some chants. They closed their eyes and held their hands out, which I followed suit with. For some reason though, I couldn't shake the fact that something about this was wrong.

"Alright, so we've said the spell for good luck. I guess the next order of business is the new recruit," Aya said.

The girl's eyes looked at my own. I then noticed Elaine smile.

"Alright, so do you know what goes...into this?" she asked me.

I shook my head.

"No." I said. " I just spent time with Aya, and she showed me things. She said this would be fun, so I decided to join in trusting her."

I didn't know why, but there was something about this which felt a bit off to say the least. Maybe it was my own personal worries about what may happen next, but then, I saw Monica smile.

"I guess you haven't been told of the initiation rite. Of course Aya would leave that out," Monica said.

"Hey, it was a lapse of judgement. Get off my fucking back," she said.

"What do you mean by...rite?" I asked.

I figured I'd at least ask. That way I kind of knew what the hell I was getting into.

They looked at me, laughing slightly. I was so confused, but then, I heard Aya speak.

"The initiation rites involve...an orgy with the other witches," she said.

An...orgy? Like all of us? I looked at her, my eyes wide with shock and surprise.

"You're not fucking around are you?" I asked her.

"I'm not. That's usually the rites that we use here. But if you don't want to do it we can—

"No....I want to," I said.

It wasn't just because of my crush on Aya, but also because well...everyone else was insanely attractive.

I was gay, and honestly...being taken by any of these women would be a treat for me, which made me flush just thinking about it. I didn't know why, but I liked the idea behind it.

"Are you sure?" Aya asked.

I nodded.

"Yeah, I'll do it," I told her.

She looked at me, smiling as she spoke.

"Good. Then get on the table. I'll start the rite," she said.

I looked at her, wondering what she was about to do, but then she pushed me onto the table, climbing up on top. We looked at one another, my face red as a tomato.

I'd be lying if I said I didn't have a crush on Aya. She was small, pretty, and she had a domineering energy right about now. I liked the idea behind it, even though I had no clue what this would mean for me. But then, moments later her mouth was on mine, kissing me passionately.

She was a forceful kisser, but I liked that about her. While she kissed me, I felt a pair of hands move towards my shirt, tugging it off. I gasped as it was pulled over my head, only for me to realize it was Elaine who was smiling as she did this.

She enjoyed the tease, and Rachel of course was right behind her, pulling off my bra with one motion.

I gasped as I realized just how quickly all of these women got me undressed. I was a bit impressed if I wasn't so damn turned on as I looked at them. Aya continued to seal my lips with a kiss, staying like this for what felt like forever. I enjoyed the touch, the tease, everything about this, and I ached for her. I wanted her so badly, and I knew that she enjoyed this too. Her hands moved around my body as each pair of the other hands were touching her. As she did this, she pulled back, saying something in Latin.

I had no fucking clue what she was talking about, but then her hands moved downwards, massaging my breasts. This felt different from a normal, massaging touch. The action felt almost exact, and I liked the way that this felt. It was...strange to say the least, but it was something that I relished in, enjoying, and desired from her. She seemed to like this too, judging from the small motions of her hips against me.

I felt the other hands against my body, realizing that all of the other women were against me, touching my body, exploring me. Monica was one of the handsier ones, touching me closer and closer towards my crotch. But Aya stopped, looking at them.

"Let me be first. Then you guys can," she said.

I flushed, wondering what exactly she meant by that. I wanted to ask, but she sealed my lips with a kiss before I could say much more.

She took my nipple in her mouth, lightly pressing and touching there, looking into my eyes as she did this. I shivered, moaning out loud, letting out a series of small cries as she continued to tease me there. Every single touch was enough to drive me mad, and I was slowly losing all semblance of control, enjoying the touch of her body, and the way she felt as I looked at her.

For a long time, she continued this, until she moved downwards, pressing her hands against my pussy. I shivered as I felt the hand against my heat, touching me, teasing me, playing with me as I looked into her eyes.

"Fuck," I said out loud.

"You good there?"

I didn't know what to say. Of course I felt good. But the fact that she seemed to know exactly where to touch me, where to make me feel good, and just how to make me lose control was hard to beat, that's for sure.

"I'm...amazing really. Just struggling to put words together," I said to her.
"Then don't worry about putting those damn words together, and just...enjoy the moment," she said.

The way she uttered those words was almost a demand, but I liked it a lot. There was a thrill that came from a woman telling me what to do.

She moved her hands downwards, between my legs, rubbing me through my pants. I let out a small moan, excitement flooding through my body as she continued to move her hands there, touching slightly.

I cried out, and soon I felt her hands move towards my pants, hooking onto them and pulling them downwards. I shivered, feeling the cold air hit there, causing me to cry out slightly. But then, before I knew it, she tossed off my pants, hiked up my legs, and I felt a tongue slither down between my legs.

I cried out, clinging to her. Her explorative tongue was so amazing, and I felt my toes curl together as I felt her tongue move towards my clit, teasing there. She explored, using her lips, mouth and hands to make me lose control. I cried out, holding onto her as she continued the onslaught of attention to me down there, making my head spin, and my body practically lose control.

I was losing my mind, excitement and need growing within me. I ached for her, and I knew that she enjoyed this as much as I did. Everything about this was just...it was so damn good, and I wanted her to continue.

She then pushed her tongue in, pressing against there, and then, moments later, I felt my body tense up, and I cried out, arching my back as I felt my orgasm hit me. I shivered, crying out with pleasure. But then, I felt something against my lips.
It was Rachel's ass, and her pussy was right there, waiting for me to take.

"Go ahead. We need to keep you quiet. Don't want you getting us in trouble and all," she said.

Fuck that's true. I knew that if I was too loud, I'd be in deep shit. I moved my tongue upwards, exploring her. The whimpering sound that she made was delightful.

I felt a hand move between my legs, teasing me there. I muffled my moans into her, holding onto her as she rides my face. I cried out between her legs, feeling the fingers touch and tease me, dragging against my folds.

I looked to see who it was, but I didn't think it was Aya. I didn't necessarily care though, because Rachel was right here, and I wanted to explore her.

She was the smallest of the group, and her pussy was tight. I pushed my tongue around, exploring every nook and cranny of her, hearing the delicious moans that came out of her as I was deep inside of her. I continued to move my lips around, exploring every part of her that I could, sliding my tongue in between her, into her, and doing what Aya did to me.

Meanwhile, the fingers that were on the outside, grazing against my clit and teasing my outer folds suddenly moved inwards. But it didn't hurt, nor was it too forceful.

Instead it felt...nice. It was relaxing to be taken like this, and I liked the feeling of this. The hand continued to lightly push into me, and I felt the thumb move against my clit.

As she did that, I started to cry out, but then Rachel's pussy was in my face.

"Keep quiet. You need to be careful," she said.

I knew I needed to be quieter, but that shit was hard. I wanted to just scream out how good this felt, but maybe that was the thrill of this. The fact that I couldn't be too loud, and that she would make me feel this way. I continued to tease and play with her pussy, pressing my tongue in, moving upwards, watching the sight in front of me.

Apparently I hit a spot, because as soon as I did that, I felt her suddenly tense up, crying out loud, holding onto me, but then her lips were silenced with a kiss. Then there was a finger that arched upwards, hitting my g spot, and as it did, I suddenly let out a shuddering moan, completely immersed in her pussy as I felt my second orgasm of the night. I was amazed, and when the finger pulled out, I moved my head around to see who it was.

It was Shana. She looked at me with a smile on her face.

"Not bad. Looks like Aya found a fun one," she said.

"Y-yeah," I said to her.

"Anyway, I have a date with a cutie," she said.

Rachel looked at her, and soon, the two of them were in the corner, making out. I laid there, completely amazed at how good I felt, when suddenly, I saw Monica there. She looked me over, licking her lips.

"You're looking delightful there," she purred.

"Really now?" I said to her with a laugh.

She came closer, holding her hands to the sides of my body, touching it slightly. I cried out, shivering as I felt her hands graze against my body, touching, teasing, and moving her longer fingernails against the side. I looked over at Shana and Rachel. Shana's hands were between Rachel's legs, touching and pressing into Rachel's tight pussy. Well maybe Rachel could take a bit more than I thought. I looked at Monica, who licked her lips.

"It's so hot watching those two get it on. It's been a while since we've done this. I know that Aya gets to take your virginity in the coven, but god it's so hard to resist. Especially with how pretty you are," she said.

My...virginity? But I wasn't a virgin. Hell I hadn't been for a long time.

She then shook her head.

"Don't matter if you are a virgin or not. With the coven...the leader takes the other woman," she said.

I was surprised by that, but it kind of made sense.

"I see."

"But...that doesn't mean I don't get to have a little bit of fun with you," she said.

She then slid herself against me, our pussies touching. She scissored herself so that our legs were together, and I simply sat there, taking all of the pleasure that I felt.

This was a first for me. I felt a little embarrassed by this, but she looked me in the eyes, shaking her head.

"Don't worry about it. I'm sure you'll be fine. And of course, Elaine can also tease you a bit too," she said.

Elaine moved her body so that the front of her pussy was right there in my face. I shivered, moving my tongue outwards, teasing her clit. But then she spread herself apart, rubbing herself there in front of me.

"Fuck you're so cute. I'm going to have a taste of you after Monica is done," she said.

I tried to reach forward, to tease her, but she simply wanted to give me a show, while Monica of course, rubbed our bodies together, both of us moaning with shock and amazement.

I didn't expect this to feel so good, but I was suddenly enveloped in pleasure, enjoying the feeling of this. I clung to Elaine, and as Monica danced her body on mine, she started rubbing herself while moving her fingers towards my clit, rubbing it too.

There was something different about the way that she touched me. She used her nail slightly, which offered a more penetrating feeling, like it was hitting me deep within my soul. I clung to her, holding her there as she started to move herself, our bodies enjoying the touch of one another, both of us excited and ready for more.

She looked me in the eyes, seeing the way I was turned on, and then, she moved herself forward, pressing against there, rubbing our clits together. As she did that, I held onto Elaine's thighs, crying out loud as I felt another orgasm.

But then Elaine silenced my sounds with a kiss, and I sat there making out with her as Monica finished, pulling away. I could see the glistening trail between the two of us, enjoying the feeling of our bodies together, both of us enjoying each other's touch.

Then, Elaine moved herself so that her fingers were right up against me. She pushed three in, dipping her tongue there, and I felt her curl them upwards, almost methodically touching me.

"Holy—"

"That's Elaine for you. She knows exactly where to make you feel good," I heard Monica say.

I didn't expect this. Her touches were on the ball, hitting every single part of me, and when she did that, I couldn't help but moan, excitement growing within me as I started to hold onto her, crying out loud and enjoying the feeling of this. I continued to move my hips, enjoying the touch, ravaging my own body, the hype and feeling of this becoming such a turn on that I didn't know how to stop.

After a few more thrusts, she angled her fingers upwards, her thumb pressing against my clit, almost pushing it in. I formed fists with my hands, feeling them ball together as I arched my back, moaning out loud as I felt the pleasure of my body as she took it and used it completely.

I ached for her, enjoying the sensation, the touch, and the feeling. But then she did it again, and I suddenly let out a guttural sound, holding back the screams that I felt.

This was just...amazing really, and I felt something shoot out as soon as I felt her touch me right then and there. She moved back, licking her dainty fingers, looking me in the eyes.

"You taste amazing," she said.

"Thanks," I said.

I felt completely spent, but I knew that it wasn't over yet. Not until the leader took me.

I looked over at Aya, who was naked now, her hand against her body, jerking off to the sight of me cumming. I looked over, and noticed that the other girls in this coven were already making out with one another. I was so hot and bothered, but also so spent, that it was a combination of both of these feelings that made me feel amazing.

Aya walked over, rubbing her clit against mine, and I let out a small cry. But before it could go anywhere, she looked at me.

"Are you ready for this?" she said.

She meant of course, the culmination of this. The sounds of moans and sex were what filled the room. I didn't expect for this to all happen, but I wasn't going to complain about it, that's for sure.

"You sure?" I asked her.

"It's not my call hun. It's yours," she insisted.

Of course it was my call. I felt a bit embarrassed, but I knew deep down that this was indeed what I wanted.

I simply nodded.

"Yes. I want this," I insisted. I knew what I wanted.

Her lips curled into that of a smile, giving me a small kiss.

"I knew you were the right one when I started talking to you in the lab that day. I just thought you were cute, but I didn't expect this much fun," she said.

I flushed, realizing she enjoyed this as much as I did. I quickly nodded, excited about what may happen next, and just what she had in store for me. There was so much excitement, so much feeling, that I knew that she was making this fun for me as well.

I didn't expect this much as well, but there was something exciting, almost thrilling, about being taken like this, used in this fashion, and enjoyed by all of these beautiful women.

I couldn't get enough.

I watched as they moved their bodies near my own, looking at me as one of them gave Aya a double sided strap on dildo. She fastened it onto her body, while sliding one side inside herself, letting out a small cry herself.

The other 2 women were in the throes of sex, and I could feel the heat rising in this place.

Maybe we were more hidden away than I thought.

Aya's hands dragged against my body, sliding downwards, massaging my hip bones, before she looked me in the eyes.

"You're beautiful. I can't wait to show you...true pleasure," she purred into my ear.

"Ahh, yes," I told her.

I wanted this as much as she did, and there was something exciting about this, something fun and extremely thrilling. She then moved her body so that she was right up against my entrance, sliding the other side of the dildo inside of me.

I grimaced slightly, surprised by how...full I felt as she did this. She pushed all the way in, looking me in the eyes as she slid herself further and further inside of me.

"There we go. Just relax," she cooed into my ear.

It was hard to truly relax, but I listened to her, completely immersed and mesmerized by the way she seemed to have complete, utter control over my body. I knew that she would take care of me, and she would make me feel good.

She soon slid herself fully into my opening, opening me up and holding me there. She then moved her body slightly, and while she filled me up completely, I let out a guttural sound of pleasure.

"You good?" she asked.

"Yea. Amazing," I said.

The way she had command over my body, combined with the sounds of the women in the background, it was all just...utterly amazing. I felt like I was under her spell, her control, and I ached for her.

She then started to move her hips, pressing in and out, in and out, and I relished in the feeling of this, enjoying the sensations that I felt as she leaned forward, grasping my breasts, teasing them from between her fingertips. I shivered, holding onto her as she continued this onslaught against my body. She was moaning with me, feeling the pleasure she was giving herself at the same time.

I knew that she was good, but I didn't expect this good. But the way she touched me was enough to drive me crazy. I started holding onto her as she arched my body, keeping it there as she pushed herself deeper and deeper into me, keeping me in place while she was grinding herself out on the other end of the dildo that had filled her up.

"There we go. Good girl," she cooed into my ear.

She pulled my knees upwards, bringing them over her shoulders, keeping them there as she thrusted deep inside me. I sat there, taking this, enjoying the sensation of this, enjoying the fact that she was also receiving pleasure from all of this, feeling completely immersed in the experience, the pleasure of it all, and the absolute fun that came out of this.

After a few more thrusts, she reached forward, rubbing me. I wanted to touch her as well, to make her feel good in other ways, but she kept my hands downwards, holding me there.

"Yes, that's good. You're getting close aren't you?" she said.

I nodded, completely shocked and surprised by this.

"Yes," I said to her, completely shocked with need and desire. I was at my limit, and she was too.

But before she finished, she looked at me, saying a few words. I had no idea what they were, but I presume it was in Latin. She then grabbed me, angling her body so that she was right up against the very edge of me, and then pushed there, hitting that sweet spot inside of me.

I cried out, shivering with delight as I came hard, holding onto her as I felt the end, the pleasure, and the orgasm that I had just completely overtaken me while feeling her being overtaken by her own orgasm. Her body tensed up with mine and we both exploded together. The sensation was like shocking waves that we were both experiencing at the same time and it felt like they had brought us closer than ever before. It felt like a true initiation into something amazing. Something I couldn't quite put words to.

It was heavenly, the pleasure was not just all mine, which made it all so much better and it was then when, after a few more thrusts, she pulled out, giving me a kiss on the lips. I enjoyed the feeling of this, and the surprise that I felt definitely was driving me crazy.

She then sat back, looking at me with a small smile on her face. I had a feeling this had something to do of course, with what just transpired.

"You good there?" she asked.

"Amazing," I breathed out, still unable to really process everything.

She smiled.

"Good. It seems like everyone else is good too," I said.

The smell of sex, and the desires of all of these women permeated through the room. I looked at her, seeing the smile on her face as I tried to process everything that happened.

"So what does this mean?" I asked her.

"It means what you want it to mean my dear. We can....invite you to our coven fully, if that's what you want. I'm sure it would be quite the experience for everyone," she said.

"Do you do this a lot?" I asked her.

"Sometimes every full moon. It depends," she said.

I didn't know why, but there was something exciting about this, and I liked the prospect of this.

I started to pause, thinking about it all, when I nodded.

"Yeah, I want to be a part of this," I said.

"Good. And I like your attitude my dear," she said.

I flushed, but then nodded.

"Thank you. I'm excited to...to make this something special for all of us," I told her.

"Yeah, it is special, and I'm sure that it's an enjoyable experience for everyone," she
purred in my ear.

I'd be lying if I said this wasn't. The fact that she made me feel this way and knew how to turn me the fuck on, and was just...perfect really, it was all so surreal, and I couldn't help but enjoy this.

"So what's next?" I asked her.

"Well, we can finish up the meeting now, but if you want...we can go get some food," she offered.

Was this a date? I had a feeling this had the vibe of a date, I just wasn't sure.

"You sure about that? Like a date?" I asked her.

Her lips curled into that of a smile.

"Of course. Like a date hun," she told me.

I beamed. I couldn't believe it! She was really asking me out like this. There was something special about this, and it definitely was something that I was happy about. I was just ecstatic to know that I could experience something this good, this much pleasure, and this much excitement from her.

"Anyway, I figure it's time for us to head back, we have to get some studying done, don't we?" she said.

"Yeah, let's get some food and then do that," I said.

The women all came back together, clothed this time, and they started to look at me. They started to say some words, and I joined in, even though I didn't really get what they were saying. All I knew was that it was in Latin, and I figured they weren't necessarily bad.

"What were you guys saying back there?" I asked her.

I didn't know what she could possibly be saying, but then she spoke.

"We were saying 'we thank you for this new addition to our coven, and we hope for a lot of moments together like this one, and a pleasurable experience for all'" she explained.

I blushed, realizing that I meant so much to them.

"You all mean this, right?" I said to her.

"Yeah, I'm really glad that we can have you here with us. It's an exciting feeling, and something that I can't help but love," she told me.

That was nice to hear. It was a pleasure to behold too. The sounds of sex, of pleasure, of excitement which came out of this....it was just amazing.

"I'm glad I can experience all of this with you," I told her.

"Well, you'll be experiencing a whole lot more too down the line," she told me.

I shivered, nodding.

"Yeah, I hope that I can," I told her.

She grabbed my hand, pulling me in, kissing me passionately.

"Now, let's go get some dinner together. I'm starving," she said. I quickly nodded, following suit, not letting go of her arm in the least., I loved being able to hold her hand.

And that's just how it all happened. I never really believed in witches or any of that, but I started to wonder if maybe this was a sign that something bigger was about to come for me. I was excited for whatever it was. It was new and exhilarating. And regardless, I would never forget the night I shared with these women, the orgy we had, and the fun that came out of this, and the excitement and need that I got to experience, not just with Aya, but with the other girls too, who taught me a whole new world of pleasure and seduction that I never experienced before.

Elena the Dom

A Femdom, Roleplay, 69 Story

Chapter 1

"Are you fucking shitting me?" I asked myself as I read the contents of the bill.

There was no way this was true. I can't believe I had a bill of this size. I clutched the paper, my red fingernails resting on it.

Another expensive electric bill. Well that, along with the student loan debts were only making things way worse. I looked at the options on how to pay this.

I could do it now and bite the bullet. However, by doing that, it meant that I'd be screwed on rent and god knows what else.

The other option was I could defer it. Again. They'd probably come after me this go around. I wondered what the best option would be here. Or even what I should do.

"Come on, think," I muttered to myself.

I needed something, anything to get out of this fucking rut. But that's easier said than done, especially when you're someone who can't even have a normal fucking paycheck. I was sick of never having enough money, always having to make sure that I could get to work and back, sacrificing food for all of this bullshit.

I was just so damn...sick of it you know?

There was a lot that was sitting in the back of my own head, a lot of problems that were only getting worse and worse for me. Should I just take the bullet for another month? Or should I look for another option.

Then, I remembered what Sadie said.

"You should join me at the dungeon. You can help Dom some of these guys. They 're such suckers, and you'll love it."

I thought about that offer. I mean, would domming a bunch of random ass dudes be worth it. I've never done it before. A lot of people always saw me as that sweet, little woman who could hold her ground of course. But being a dom? That sounded like so much work.

But maybe, that's the type of work I was looking for. Being a dom would mean of course that I'd get to have control over men, tease them, and have my way with them too. But I didn't know what guys would want.

How mean could I be? I tried to do a bit of research on this, scouring the internet and looking for something, anything that could give me more information on how to do this. But all that came up were trashy articles talking about shit that I already knew.

I wanted the real answers, and I wanted to find out about this too.

I looked at the options. It was kind of early, that's for sure, but I definitely wanted to see what was up.

I got my shit together, heading out to the dungeon, and I figured this could be something fun to do.

There was also the fact that it could help me get my mind of things. Maybe it was for me. Maybe it would be the worst thing that I'd get to do. But who knows, maybe things would work itself out.

I put on a pair of black heels, a short black skirt, and a black shirt that cut off at my midriff. I put my black hair in an updo, coating my face in makeup to make me look more seductive. I thought I looked hot at least.

I guess there's a first for everything, right?

I walked over to the car, getting to the club, enjoying the feeling of the night, the thrill of this, and the excitement that flowed through me.

When I got there, I saw Sadie at the entrance, looking around. When we locked eyes, her blue ones lit up.

"Yo! You're here," she said, surprise obvious in her voice.

"I told you I would come out eventually. And well…I need the help," I told her.

"What do you mean?"

"I have another one of those bills," I told her.

"Oh shit, I'm sorry Elena. Anything I can do to help?" she asked.

"Well, I think I just…need to have some fun tonight,"
I told her.

"There you go. It's not that hard. Plus, I'm guessing
Christina is at her dad's?" she asked.

"Yah she's with him," I said.

And thank god she was. I did like Christina, but she
definitely made things a lot harder. But maybe I can
provide a better life for her down the road. She was
my kid, and while she was of school age, it really
didn't make things any easier for the both of us.

"Anyway, you want me to hook you up with someone
tonight?" she asked.

I flushed, wondering what she meant by that.

"What do you mean?"

"I have a couple of regulars I haven't been able to
say. They're cool with me having them go with other
people, and I told them I had a really great one for
them. Maybe you can show them a good time," she
purred.

I couldn't believe this.

"How much?" I asked. I wasn't going to do this shit
for free.

"Well, let me show you the going rate for what one
of the guys was willing to pay," she offered.

She flipped through the little pocketbook that she
had, showing me the numbers that were there.

I almost shat myself at the numbers. For one night, 500 bucks. That could get me out of a jam and then some. I couldn't believe this, and for a second, I didn't know what to say.

"You're...you're serious?" I said to her.

"This is what they normally pay, yeah. It's why I'm a stay-at-home mom you know. I do this to help pay for my daughter. And they know that I have kids. They love it," Sadie said.

So, it's okay to do this while having a kid. I'd never really gotten a chance to explore the dominating side of me. When I was married to Dave, he was anything but submissive. He always wanted to dominate, even when I tried to take control.

But now, I get to explore something more.

"You...sure about this one?" I asked her.

"What do you mean?' of course I'm sure," she said.

I started to put it all together, letting all of this seep on in. They would pay me this much.

"By the way, here's what they kind of like. Perhaps you could help them experience this," she said.

She gave me another piece of paper, with a couple of notes written down next to the client's name, who was called Brayden.

Feet, ball busting, nurses. I just need someone to dominate me while also caring for me.

I thought this guy was some sort of weirdo. Just reading the laundry list of fetishes made me nervous. I turned to her, and she smiled.

"Don't you worry. I'm sure this will be fine. If you do a good job, there's a lot more where that came from," she pointed out.

A lot more than this? Jesus, what kind of clients did she have?

I quickly nodded, heading on inside. I saw a series of costumes out, picking up the nurse uniform and tossing it on, keeping the black leather panties and heels. I knew it was door number two, so I went down there, knocking on the door.

"Come in mistress," the man said. His voice was hesitant, like he was scared of me coming in.

"I'm coming in no matter what," I said to him.

I opened the door, seeing him sitting there. He was in a pair of black boxer shorts, his hands already up on the nightstand, clinging to some cuffs. They were attached to the bed.

For the first time in a long time, I felt nervous. I'd never done something like this before. In fact, I had no idea what would come out of this.

"You're Brayden, aren't you?" I said.

"Yes. And what should I call you?"

I hesitated, almost saying my real name, when I shook my head.

"Mistress is fine. And you better not call me anything else. Or else—"

I grabbed my foot, putting it right up against his cock.

"I'll crush your fucking balls underneath my heels," I said to him. Hearing those words out of me felt so damn foreign, like I was doing something wrong. But then, I heard the moan as I dug into there slightly.

"O-okay mistress. I believe you will," he said.

"Good. So today you asked for a nurse, right?" I said to him.

"Yes, I need someone to take care of me. I'm tired of taking care of others and—"

I grabbed the thermometer, shoving it into his mouth hard. He shut up, and I checked it.

"Good, now that'll keep your mouth shut. You want this nurse to do her job, right? And she will, as long as you stay quiet, and you follow my instructions. I'll give you everything that you need to get nice and healthy," I purred.

He nodded, his eyes widening. For the first time in a while, I felt strong. I felt confident, and when I checked the temperature, I pulled it out.

"Looks healthy. But you said you had some pain. Where was it?" I asked him.

"My stomach and—"

I pushed my heel into his stomach, causing him to moan and cry out in pain.

"Ahh!" he said.

"I can help with that stomach pain. How about this?" I said, lightly moving about. I continued to press down there, watching his eyes widen, and a moan escape him.

I continued to touch, to tease him with my shoe, and I didn't expect him to enjoy this so much.

"So, I heard you like feet, right? Maybe you can take care of this mistress's feet. Since of course you're still a bit sick, aren't you? I said to him.

"Y-yes mistress," he said.

I dug the heel right into there and he extended his tongue, licking the tips of the shoe, then over to the heel.

I then pulled the heel off, and he began to service my toes, licking, teasing, and touching them. It was so weird, because I was never one to enjoy feet, but seeing this man become so enamored in this was fun.

But I wasn't going to let him feel satisfaction. In fact, I wanted to see him squirm a bit more. I looked at the obvious erection in his pants, standing at attention and waiting for me. I smiled as I enjoyed this man's reaction.

"Look at your pathetic cock, already getting hard for me. I see how it is," I said, stepping on his cock. He let out a low groan as I continued this. But then, I pulled away. I looked into his eyes, smiling.

"Now...what is it that you need?" he said.

"I need...medicine. I need your medicine," he said.

"Ohhh really now? You're going to need to beg for it," I told him.

I stepped down on him once again, hearing him groan in slight agony and pleasure, and then spoke.

"Please, give this to me now!" he said.

I laughed, watching his pathetic body squirm in response. I pulled back, looking into his eyes.

"Well now, maybe I could give you the medicine that you desire...for a price," I told him.

"Please, anything mistress," he said.

I looked at him, smiling in contentment.

"Turn around. Turn on the bed," I said to him.

He quickly did so, his ass in the air. He did have a nice butt, very spankable, and I saw the crop that was there.

I grabbed the crop, rubbing it against the tip of his backside. He let out a small moan, and I smiled. And then, I pulled back, pressing it there, slapping him slowly, and then a little bit harder.

"Come now, you need to beg for your medicine," I purred into his ear.

"Arrgh yes, please mistress give me this," he cried out.

There was a thrill that I enjoyed. I saw the flogger in the corner, grabbing it and placing it right over his backside.

"What was that I heard?"

"Yes mistress! Give me more!" he screamed out.

There was that excitement, that need, and that desire which came from all of this. I readied the flogger, hitting him straight on the backside, hearing the grunts that came from him. I looked at him, seeing his butt arch up slightly, and I couldn't help but laugh at him.

God, he looked so damn pathetic, but there was something fun about this man being on this level with me, so turned on and used like this. There was an excitement which came forth about it, and as I hit him once more, he let out a cry.

"Now...what was it that you wanted?" I said to him, rubbing my hand against his hard backside.

"Please mistress...I want you to...to take me," he said.

"Really now? What was that?" I said, rubbing a gloved hand against him. Just seeing him shiver like that was a thrill I couldn't get enough of.

"Please mistress. Just...take me please," he said.

I wanted to see him squirm. He'd be the first one.

"You want your medicine then?" I asked.

"Yes! I want the medicine. Please," he begged.

Seeing him come apart like this sent a thrill through me that I didn't even expect. I slapped his ass hard once more, hearing him shiver with delight.

"Well, I'm sure that you can get your medicine then...just give me a moment," I said.

I turned him around, seeing his hardened cock there. I touched it, grabbing it hard, watching him cry out. Having a man under my control like this felt so damn different. But man was it fun.

I rubbed him at first, hearing him let out a series of small cries as I did this, and there was something fun and thrilling about this, about watching him just completely lose all semblance of control like this. For a long time, I simply teased him around, watching him tense up, moaning.

"Please mistress, just one more," he said.

"Ah ah. You can't tell me what to do. Or else you'll get punished," I said, lightly grasping his cock again. He shivered, crying out in slight shock and surprise.

"Please mistress I need it! I need your medicine," he said.

Hearing the agonized cries of this man sent something through me. Was it...a feeling of excitement? Was it the fact that I had control over this man, and there was nothing that he could do to stop me?

Perhaps it was, and in truth, I liked hearing him lose control over every single touch, losing his mind at the sheer mention of my touches, the teases, the pleasure that this man had.

"Well since you asked nicely, I think I can give you your medicine. But only because you've been such a good boy," I teased, hearing the whimpering sound of approval from this man. I moved my panties off to the side, moving downwards until my pussy was right over his face.

"But you'll also need to take care of me too. That's how the medicine works," I teased him.

He groaned, pushing his cock upwards, and soon, I rested myself downwards, sitting on his face. He let out a small, muffled cry as I started grinding my hips there, watching him tense up. I took the tip of his cock into my mouth, sucking on it, moving down against it, hearing him groan out.

I smothered my pussy on his face, my juices coating his mouth and face. This was a thrill that I couldn't get enough of, and watching him groan and move around in agony was fun, and yet I could also see the nervousness that was there, and the way that he seemed to just completely lose it all as I did this.

I loved it. I knew that he liked it too, but there was also that feeling of desire and raw need, that seemed to only drive me closer and closer to the edge as well.

I continued to move my hips against him, hearing him groan with delight. I took him further down my mouth, finally getting it to the base of my throat. I moved my tongue, licking the shaft, hearing the sounds of desire that came out from this.

"Fuck," he muffled under me.

I pushed my hips downwards, letting out a series of small cries.

"I'll let you cum when you're done with me," I said to him.

He worked his magic, his tongue moving outwards, roving against my body, making me shiver with delight, moaning slightly in response to everything that was going on. This brought forth a feeling and thrill that I wasn't expecting. But I started grinding my hips, hearing him groan with pleasure at the sensation of this.

"Yes. That's a good boy! Continue," I cried out, enjoying this way more than I expected to. He worked his magic, still touching, teasing, and moving his lips around as much as he could, savoring me.

When he stuck his tongue in, pressing into me and upwards, I suddenly felt that sudden urge surge through me. I pressed my face down, rubbing it there, grinding against him as I took his cock in my mouth, moving my lips up and down.

"Yes," I said out loud. I was so damn close, and he knew this too. I knew he enjoyed this as much as I did, and with every little touch, every way his tongue poked into me, turning me on and touching me, I knew that I was near my limit.

After a few more moments, he pressed his tongue upwards, causing me to tense up, letting out a small cry as I pressed my hips there, coming hard as I suffocated him. In response, he let out a barely audible groan as he came against my lips. I quickly swallowed it all, moving off of him.

The man was spent, and my lips curled into that of a smile.

"There we go," I said out loud.

I moved my hand to his thighs, touching it slightly.

"That's a good boy. Now be good. I'll come back and give you the medicine you need anytime," I purred in his ear.

He let out a small cry before laying there, completely spent and amazed by this. I undid the restraints and slowly got the blindfold off. He looked at me, smiling.

"There we go," he told me.

"You're good. Do you need anything?" I asked.

That's part of the dom lifestyle. Making sure that every one of them was taken care of.

"Yeah, I'm good," he told me.

I beamed.

"Great. Well, you're free to leave whenever," I said.

After he was done, I cleaned up the room and then went outside. My friend looked at me with a smile.

"So, did you enjoy it Elena?" she asked.

I beamed.

"Did I? That shit was so much fun! And I mean...I liked that I got a little something out of it too," I told her.

"Yeah, that's the fun of being a professional dominatrix. So, if you want to, you're always welcome to come back," she offered.

Was this the big moment I'd been looking for? Was this the gig that would spur me to do something different with myself, with my life?

Perhaps it was.

My lips curled into that of a smile as I thought about Sadie's offer.

"You know, you might be onto something," I told her.

"Yeah, I know I am. Well, you're welcome to come back tomorrow. Oh, and here's the money from that guy. He's a pretty big businessman, which is why he wears the hood," she said.

A couple of hundreds were thrown into my hand. After counting it, it was nearly a grand! I got a grand just from being a bit of a bully to a random guy?

Something about this seemed almost too good to be true, and I felt that excitement and desire grow within me.

"You know, you may be onto something with this," I told her.

"I know that I am. I've been doing this long enough. I guess I'll see you tomorrow," she said.

And when I left, that's when I realized it. I enjoyed this, far more than I thought I'd enjoy something of this caliber. I mean, I did like teasing guys, but the fact that I could get paid for it, and it was good money was almost too good to be true. But here I was, thinking about all of this, and the realization of it all.

It awoke something within me, and I had a feeling this would drive me to make other decisions, ones that would be different from the life I led before.

Chapter 2

That's what began my descent into being a femdom.

At first it was just one situation where I ended up choosing to mess around with one guy for fun and giggles.

But now...it's something more.

It turned into something different, and when I walked in today, seeing that he wanted me to roleplay a cop, I certainly felt a whole burst of excitement there. The thrill of roleplaying different types of characters that would otherwise not happen....it was quite fun.

I walked over to the entrance, seeing Sadie there. This time she was in a leather dress that hugged her body, and straps that hugged her thighs, showing a teeny bit of the extra thickness that was there. She looked hot, but the smile that she had on her face said everything.

"So, ready to rock and roll tonight?" she teased.

"Born ready," I replied.

"Good. This is your next client. I guess he likes cops. Maybe he's wanted to be dominated by one," she said.

I looked at what he wanted. I flushed seeing the words that were there.

Pegging.

I'd never done this before. I thought about this, noticing that she was curious about my response.

"Something wrong?" she asked.

"I've never pegged someone before," I admitted with a reddened face.

"Oh, that's easy! Trust me on this, guys love this type of shit. It's clear that he's probably use to this too. So, don't worry," she replied.

I wasn't planning on worrying.

I liked this. It awoke a feeling of power within me, something I wasn't used to. Maybe it was the fact that I got to experience something so fun, so magical, and so different from the norm. but also...it was that feeling of power, something that I definitely enjoyed and craved.

"That sounds like fun," I told her.

"This guy loves that shit. He's so into women taking control of him, so I imagine he'll like what you have planned for him," she told me.

I hoped that he did.

I got into the cop uniform, a tight leather skirt, and a shirt that showcased my cleavage in an ample manner. There was something fun about dressing up, about letting go and experiencing the fun of this. I looked at the door, preparing myself for what I was about to see.

When I opened the door, I saw a man sitting there prone on the ground, his ass in the air. He shivered with delight.

"I'm sorry officer I—"

I took my heel, digging it into his back.

"You have the right to remain silent. So, what's it going to be? You're coming with me to jail? Or…. maybe you want me to treat you a little differently than the others that I nab," I said.

I dug the heel in, watching him grimace, but there was also that moan that escaped his voice as I continued this.

"Please mistress, I'll do anything," he said.

"Anything I say? Even of course…submitting to me?" I said with a laugh.

"Yes! I want that mistress," he told me.

"Well then aren't we the feisty one. Fine, I guess I can take you up on this offer," I pointed out.

I took the heel, walking on him. He let out a low, guttural sound that made me excited, shivering with delight, enjoying the feeling of this man against me. There was something fun about taking a man like this, making him mine, and watching him submit.

I certainly could see that he was enjoying this too. I looked down, seeing his cock standing at attention.

"Look at you, all turned on by my heels! I can't believe this. I'm surprised you can even say things. How are you feeling? Like you're under my control?"

I said, grabbing the chains that he was in, pulling on them.

Ahh yes! I'm under your control," he replied.

"Heh, good. I'm glad we can see things like this. Because look at your pathetic ass. Such a poor soul, only here to be used as a cocksleeve and nothing more," I said.

I pressed my heel against him once again. But that's when I saw it.

His tight little hole. It twitched as I did this, making me chuckle.

"Just look at your pathetic ass. You're sitting here, ass in the air, turned on by the sheer mention of my foot against your hard cock. Wow, what a pathetic little bitch," I told him.

"Yes, I'm a pathetic bitch mistress. Please just—"

I stepped on him again, this time slapping his ass as well. He let out a small yelp, twitching in response to my motions.

"Silence! You have the right to remain silent. We're not done here," I told him.

I then moved over towards the array of toys, seeing a variety of different dildos. There were also ones specifically for the strap-on, which were quite bigger than I imagined.

Would he really enjoy this?

There was also a double-ended one. I considered that, but it was one of the bigger ones.

"Let's see how well you handle my treatment," I told him.

"Is this punishment?"

I gave him a long, hard slap on the ass, causing him to let out a yelping sound.

"You're goddamn right it is," I spat in his face.

He let out a whimper as I began to lube up the first dildo, something that's pretty small and tame. I figured this was something that most people could handle.

I spread his cheeks apart, sliding the toy inside. He let out a small, garbled sound, but then a moan as I began to press it in and out.

"Look at you, all turned on by this," I told him.

I continued to press in and out, watching his eyes widen, and the moans that he had escaped his mouth. It was hot to watch, that's for sure. I continued to tease him, but then I pulled it out slightly.

"You seem to be taking this very well. But this isn't something you should be enjoying you little worm," I told him, smacking him hard against the ass.

"No! I don't want to enjoy this! I want you to hurt me! make me pay for my crimes," he screamed out.

"You're goddamn right I'm going to make you pay," I said to him, spitting in his face.

Before I knew it, I had a bigger dildo in my hands, one that was about eight inches, but a bit girthier. I shoved it inside, at first slow and steady, but as he took it, I pressed it in a whole lot harder, watching him cry out with pleasure as I continued to move it deep within him.

"Look at this slutty little hole, taking this toy like this. My, I can't believe you haven't been taken sooner. I'm surprised, you may be liking this," I told him.

He grimaced, letting out a small cry of pleasure as I continued to move the toy in and out, watching him shiver with delight, and the sounds that it made turning me on immensely. I smirked, watching his eyes widen as I continued this, enjoying the sounds that he made, the squelching that was heard as I shoved the toy in and out, and the excitement that came out of his mouth.

He was turned on, but I also heard the slight grunts of pain. He enjoyed the torture though, given how hard his cock was, and how he didn't use the safe word that I'd been given by Sadie to continue this.

"You like that you little slut? Me just assailing your hole?" I told him.

"Yes! Give me more! I crave it," he screamed out.

"Heh, look at you. You're a fucking mess," I said.

I grabbed the whip that was in my belt, unclipping it and then hitting him directly with it. He let out a small, sensual cry as I did this, whipping him again and again.

"Yes! Give this to me! I'm bad and—"

I wrapped the gag around his mouth.

"Quiet down. I didn't tell you to speak," I said, whipping him hard one last time for good measure. The arch of his back, the cry that he uttered, it was driving me insane.

And that's when I decided to do it.

I took the dildo out, watching him whimper in response to this. I looked at him, seeing the way his body shook slightly, the little sound that came out of his lips, the ache that was clearly there.

He was enjoying this. Probably more than I should be letting him.

"I never told you that you could enjoy this!" I said to him, smacking him hard.

"Ahh! Yes, I'm not. You're using me like the bad boy that I am. Please, just use me," he said.

I looked at the way his hole stretched out, looking almost inviting to me. I never really thought about pegging a guy like this, but seeing how he just completely lost all semblance of control the moment I started to tease him was fun.

"Fine, because you're already so turned on, and you're asking nicely, I will," I told him.

I moved over to the cabinet, trying to figure out which toy I wanted to use. There were a variety, but the double-ended one was calling me. That way I could have my fun too while teasing this man.

"Please officer! Just use me. I promise I'll never do it again," he cried out.

I didn't expect this to be so hot to me. My tits were perked, my pussy wet, and soon, before I knew it, I could feel that ache growing within, that need growing as well.

I moved my body so that my back was right up against his. I lubed it up—I wasn't that mean of course. I wanted to make sure that this was something that he would enjoy too.

"Alright, ready? This is your punishment," I said.

"Please officer! Give me the punishment," he told me.

Such a pathetic man, looking all turned on. I slid myself slowly into him, feeling him twitch and quiver slightly, a little bit of resistance as I entered into his pucker.

"What's the matter? Can't handle it? I can always pull out, and then you'll have to get your punishment a different way," I teased.

"No! I need this. I want you to punish me. Please," he said, the cries of pleasure obvious in his voice.

"There we go," I said, feeling the resistance diminish slightly. This would be enough, right? I quickly moved myself so that I was deep inside, hearing him groan out loud.

In truth, this was turning me on too. The fact that I could feel him inside, and the way the toy moved against me was quite fun. I enjoyed this, feeling like

I was in control, that I could take the lead, and that he was definitely at the mercy of my touches.

"There we go. So easy to work with. Such a good little bad boy," I told him, sliding myself in and out of him, listening to him cry out in response to me. The thrill of this was something that I enjoyed, and there was an excitement that grew within me as I started to feel him move against me, fucking the dildo as well. I tried to hold back my own moans, but the truth was, this was turning me on immensely too.

"You're so good at this, such a good pet. It surprises me," I told him.

"I'm only aiming to be the best that I can be for you mistress. I know that it's a lot, but I want to be the best that I can, to make you feel good too," he said.

"Good, as you should," I said.

I gripped his hips, moving them up and down, pushing them against me. as he did that, I angled the toy a little bit, feeling the moans escape my own mouth. I was aroused, enjoying all of this.

I moved the angle of this a little bit differently, feeling like I was on top of the world as I did this. It was then when, after a few more thrusts, I pressed deep within, watching him cry out, and the spurt of cum shoot out of him.

I felt my own orgasm hit me, feeling the toy press against my g-spot, causing me to cry out, feeling my hips move, pressing into his prostate, watching the cum fly out, hitting the floor there.

I pulled back, catching my breath.

"Good job. So good at being an obedient little slut," I told him.

"I-I try to be," he told me.

"Tell you what, clean that up, and maybe I'll let your pathetic ass go," I said.

I moved his face down, forcing the man to clean up his own seed, causing me to smile in excitement. There was something fun about this, about making him lose all semblance of control like this, that I couldn't get enough.

He cleaned it all up, and when he looked at me, a little bit nervous, I laughed.

"Look at you. Such a mess. Go ahead, you're free. You get off with a warning, but if I catch you doing this again...your punishment may not be as good as you think," I told him.

"Y-yes," he said.

I walked out, smiling as I pulled the double-ended dildo out of me, sighing.

"Damn that was fun," I said.

There was an excitement that came from this, a feeling of power that grew within me. I could definitely get used to this.

I felt like I was slowly becoming more and more of a degenerate when it came to turning on men and making them feel good. But who knows, maybe it's just the nice paycheck too.

When I got out, Sadie looked at me with a smile.

"There you are," she said to me.

"Yeah, sorry, it took a little longer than I expected. That guy was a bit of a tougher nut to crack," I told her.

"Well, whatever you did, he loved it. He gave you a bonus," she said.

She handed me a bunch of stacks.

"This is two grand," I told her.

"Yeah, because you gave him pleasure. Us doms can make a ton of money out of this, and the guys here are pathetic little worms, I'm sure they'll love it if someone took them and used them like this," she told me.

I didn't expect there to be such a market for this.

"I'll take on more clients," I finally decided.

"You sure? I know it's a lot, given your daughter and all and—"

"No, it's fine. This gives her a good life. Why would I deny my child that," I said.

I was a mother sure, but I also knew that if I continued this, I could be the best parent possible to my kid.

"Very well, I'll give you some more clients. I'm sure this will be fun," she said.

Chapter 3

"Come on you have to beg for it. Beg for me to sit on your cock," I said, rubbing the whip against the tip, coiling it there.

"Please mistress, do this. I've been a naughty boy. I ate the chocolate chip cookies," he said.

I whipped him again, watching him cry out in pleasure as I started to laugh.

"You are a little bit. You were a very naughty boy, eating your mistress's cookies like that. I thought you were the gardener, but here you are, thinking that you own the place or something," I told him.

"No mistress! I'm sorry," he cried out.

I smacked him again with the whip, hearing him shiver and cry out.

"Now, will you promise to never do it again?" I asked him.

I rested my fingers on his delicate chest, touching, teasing his nipples by pulling on the clamps. It's something special that he liked.

"Yes mistress! I promise ahh!" he said, crying out and arching his back as I continued to tease him with the chain.

I smiled, enjoying this as I watched him become a mess in front of me, completely turned on and enjoying the feeling of this.

"Good boy. I guess now that you've suffered enough, your mistress can give you what you want. But I'm going to put a condom on there, so you don't fill your mistress's pussy with your cum," I told him.

I grabbed his dick hard, watching him tense up, moaning out loud in response.

"T-that's fine mistress! Whatever you want," he said.

"Heh, good boy," I said.

I watched him whimper as I got off, grabbing a tight rubber as I started to move it over his cock. I started to see him shiver as I pushed it on there, letting the elastic of it bounce back, causing him to let out a small whimper of both pleasure and pain.

"Look at you. Such a goddamn pathetic mess," I told him.

"Yes, I am! I'm a pathetic mess mistress! Please just...just take me," he said.

"Wow, you really are over here begging for this. What a pathetic little bitch," I said.

This was one of my favorite clients, because no matter what I did, he always sounded like he was seconds away from orgasming all over the damn place. I moved my hips onto each side of him, sliding myself down on his shaft, letting out a small cry.

It was fun teasing guys like this. As they sat there, at my command, their cocks hard as I teased them and played with them. Dominating men was a whole lot of fun, and I slowly changed my career to doing this full-time.

I started shifting my hips, going slowly at first, watching him lose control as he started to tense up. I then stopped.

"I will tell you when you can cum," I snapped at him.

"O-okay mistress," he said.

I giggled, moving my hips, watching him tense up, crying out as I slowly, languidly let his cock sit deep within me. I watched him tense as I saw him cry out, trying his best to thrust his hips up, but I stopped him.

"I didn't tell you that you could do that," I said, slapping him.

"Ahh mistress!" he said.

I then started to move faster and faster. He struggled to hold back the delicious sounds that came from him, and I couldn't help but feel the surge of power, excitement, and fun that came out of this.

I continued to thrust my hips up and down, watching him tense up, screaming out.

"Please mistress I can't hold it back any longer! Please let me cum," he cried out. I watched him, smiling in excitement as I held onto his hips.

"Do you want to cum? Do you really want to cum?" I asked him.

"Yes," he breathed out.

'Really now? You've got to convince me better than that," I said with a giggle.

"Ahh mistress! Please let me cum!" he screamed out.

I looked into his eyes, seeing the need, the pleasure, the desire that came out of this.

"Well, I guess since you asked nicely and all, I'll let you cum," I said.

I then pushed my fingers away, watching him cry out, groaning as he moved his hips. He hit that one spot, which made me gasp, holding it for a second, and then I let out a small moan too, cumming there.

He then groaned, the cum spraying out, the warm sensation hitting me. This was nice, and I didn't have to worry about diseases or pregnancy of course. It was fun to just tease him like this, watching him lose all of the control that he struggled to hold onto as I thrust in deep.

"There you go," I said.

When he was done, I moved off of him, undoing the restraints.

"You good to go? Because if so, the mistress has another appointment right now," I told him.

"Yes mistress," he finally managed to breathe out.

I smirked, enjoying how much of a mess he was. I then watched him struggle as I left the room.

"There you are again? How was this customer?" Sadie asked.

"It was fun. He was easy to mess with," I told her.

"Good. He paid decently to. Check that out," she said.

Another couple grand.

"This is great. Definitely will help with my daughter," I told her.

"Well, that's what's so fun about this. You can do whatever you want, and you can have a bunch of fun while doing so," she said.

That's kind of what I enjoyed about this. It was the fact that I could be myself, and tease men. There was a thrill that came from that.

"Well, I think I'm going to head in, work with the next customer tonight," I told her.

"Good. I think they'll enjoy that," she replied.

And that was it. It was time for me to move onto the next one, the next customer, who would make things even more fun. I felt the excitement and need grow within me but I had no clue what would happen next.

All I did know was that I was ready to be a dom, ready to make men squirm, and I loved that I could make money doing just that, enjoying the aspects of this that I could enjoy too.

The Massage Therapist
A Tantric Sex, 69, BDSM, Wife Swapping Story

Chapter 1

"How was meeting up with Casey?" my husband Arnold asked.

"It was good. He helped me with that crick in my neck. Really did me some good," I told Arnold.

"Yeah, it was nice meeting up with Melonie too," he replied.

My husband and I were in a swinging "Wife swapping" sort of thing. He would go with Casey's wife Melonie, while I would go with Casey to explore some of the sexual aspects that Arnold normally didn't really like.

Arnold was a little bit older than I was, and a traditional man. He had short blonde hair, blue eyes, and was of average build. He was a man that I'd fallen for, and we've still been close to one another, I definitely felt like this whole wife swapping thing was good for both of us.

He was seeing Melonie, who was Casey's wife. Melonie was cute. Small, thick, and a redhead with green eyes. She kind of looked like me, albeit a little bit younger than myself. Which wasn't necessarily wrong or anything, but it's clear that Arnold did have a spot in his heart for the more traditional types, something that I couldn't totally fill.

Meanwhile, I'd been seeing Casey. Casey was much different. Between the array of tattoos on his arms, his long black hair, and his brown eyes, he was the antithesis of Arnold. However, he was muscular, and although he looked like a tough guy, he was definitely very sweet, and he was a massage therapist in town, one of the most popular out there.

This wife swapping thing began about a year ago, when he suggested it to me drunkenly regarding Melonie. We agreed, and I saw Casey. That's when things changed. We soon got to learn one another, and it was a different kind of game for us. Rather than it just being something vanilla, there was the fun of variety, something that I didn't necessarily get with Arnold, and something that, deep down I did utterly miss in a strange way.

It was odd, but our first-time swapping was...different; it awakened a whole new world for me.

Arnold just wanted the thrill of having someone who wasn't his wife. It was strange to me, but he was the one who asked about it. I, of course, was cool with just being with Casey.

Casey and I were old friends. In fact, we almost ended up together, but our differing interests pulled us apart. But that didn't stop me from feeling a surge of excitement as I thought about the fact that I'd get to see him again, his beautiful cock penetrating me and the fun that we'd get to have.

"So.... when are you two meeting up again?" Arnold asked, looking me over.

"This Friday. He told me to meet up at his office. Not sure why though," I told him.

I think it's because of what we discussed the week before after we had sex, lying in bed together. Sure, Arnold and I still had an awesome relationship, but the pillow talk with Casey was a bit different.

"So...is there anything you want to try?" Casey asked me, touching the tips of my thighs.

"I don't know. I've been reading a bit about tantra. I don't really know much about it, but I'm curious about it," I told him.

Tantric sex was something I tried to bring up to Arnold a couple of times, but he just thought it was some weird sort of sex thing and wasn't cool with it. I tried to explain to him that it was something that was a bit different, but I guess he just wasn't feeling it.

"I've been reading up on tantra too. And I can give you a tantric massage, and maybe we can try tantric sex too," he purred.

Would that even work? I flushed, thinking about this. I don't know what Arnold would say if I tried it without him, but we were in this wife swapping thing, and he was boning Melonie whenever I was with him. I figured it was something that we'd get to explore down the road.

"Do you think that you can teach me? Or at least show me?" I asked him.

"Sure! I've been doing some research on this. I offered Melonie a chance to try it, but she didn't seem all that interested in it either. It's weird, because we ended up marrying two people incredibly vanilla, when we're not," he told me.

That's what I always found strange too. It wasn't the fact that they were vanilla, but it was how it ended up like this.

Still, I sat there, my eyes on his.

"Yeah, I'd like that," I told him.

"Good. Then that settles it. Next Friday we'll meet up, and we can see what this tantra is all about," he said.

I beamed.

"I'd love that. But first...why don't we take care of that," I said, pointing to the obvious erection in his pants. He gave me a small smirk, his blue eyes looking into my green ones.

"Sure, I'd love that," he told me.

I soon moved so that my pussy was right in his face, covering him with my juices. He extended his tongue, the pink muscle moving out, exploring my folds, teasing the tip of my clit. I shivered, realizing he knew exactly where to go with this, and the pleasure that this was giving me.

"Fuck this is pretty good," I told him.

"I told you it'd be fun. Besides, what's the point of sex without a little bit of...exploration," he told me.

I smiled.

"Sure, you can definitely explore me all you like," I told him.

"And that's exactly what I plan to do," he purred.

I shivered, knowing this was exactly what he wanted. He continued to tease his tongue there, moving it around, and I soon pressed my lips to the tip of his cock, teasing the very edges of it, watching his eyes widen with rapt delight as I took him further and further down, feeling his shaft fill up my mouth.

That's also something that Casey had over Arnold. He was much thicker. While Arnold was a little bit longer, Casey made up for it in girth, so it was two different instances. I started to move my lips all the way to the base, feeling it graze against the back of my throat, enjoying the sensation of this as I continued to press against there, thrusting my lips all the way down, feeling him there.

"Fuck," he said, groaning as he thrust his hips upwards.

"You like that?" I said with a smile.

"I'm loving it," he told me.

I started to gasp against his cock, feeling it hit the back of my throat. I continued to move my lips against him, up and down, up and down, sucking him off without any reason to stop. He held my *hips, exploring me, thrusting his tongue deep into me, pressing against me, hearing me cry out, tensing up and enjoying the sensation of this.*

"Fuck," I said, tensing up, feeling the pleasure of my orgasm as it hit me.

He then pressed his hips upwards, hitting the back of my throat relentlessly. He then groaned, his cock tensing, and then the release hitting my mouth. I swallowed the salty mixture, enjoying the taste, looking at him as I moved off, a smile on my face.

"How was that?" I said.

"Amazing really," he said.

"As it should be," I replied.

We sat down, enjoying the warm touch of one another. While Arnold was a lot more vanilla, Casey was fun to get those kink tendencies out, and to try something a bit different. That of course, would involve tantric massage, and maybe tantric sex.

There was that feeling of desire, of excitement, of need that grew within me at the thought of this, and I couldn't help but feel excited for what was to come.

I thought about the conversation we had that night, remembering the fun we had, what we enjoyed, and what we planned to try out the next time we saw one another. I looked at Arnold, who seemed curious.

"Honey, I think I'm going to try something new with Casey. That's okay, right?"

"It's kink-related isn't it?" he asked.

"Yeah, it is," I said.

"That's fine. Just be safe. And maybe you can show me when you get back to me," he said.

"Of course. But only if you learn something new from Melonie and want to try it with me," I said.

He pulled me in, kissing me passionately and I hungrily took his lips against mine. Sure, he was vanilla, but there was something nice about having the stability of this relationship right here, waiting for me, and something I could never let go of, no matter what happened next.

Chapter 2

I felt a bit of nervousness as I started to realize the day was getting closer. I wondered what would transpire here between Casey and I.

When I left the house, saying goodbye to Arnold, he gave me a kiss. I felt an excitement grow. I wanted to feel the excitement with him too, but I figured this would be something that I'd learn from Casey first.

When I got to the massage parlor, he was already closed up for the day, which was good. I figured that he'd be busy till late, but I guess not, which made things a little bit easier for us. When I got to the doorway, seeing him there, he gave me a small smile.

"There you are Katie," he said to me.

I smiled, feeling his eyes glaze over my body. I wore a simple black skirt with a blue sweater, seeing his eyes dance over my curves. There was something fun about this, seeing the way his body, mind, and eyes continued to dance over me.

"Hey yourself. So, are you ready to begin?" I asked him.

"Course. I've been working on the technique. Hopefully, I can make you feel magical," he said to me.

I followed him to the room, and he soon looked at me.

"First thing that I want you to do, is to get naked, and wear only this robe. I'm going to give you a massage first. Just a general one, help with the nerves and such," he said.

"Alright," I replied.

He left the room, and I took off my clothes, putting the white cotton robe on. I looked around, flushing at the realization that this was how we were going to do this.

I laid down on the table, feeling him walk in, closing the door behind him.

"Now, let's start with a simple massage. That way you can relax, and I don't know, I just want to make sure that you feel good too," he told me.

"Thanks. I do appreciate that," I told him.

He looked into my eyes, and then I put my head down. His large hands started from the top of my back, near my shoulders, slowly massaging the muscle tissue there. It felt really good, and it was enjoyable to me. I shivered, letting out a small sigh of contentment as he continued this touch.

"You feel good?" he asked.

"Amazing really. It's nice to get a massage period. I've been meaning to work out the kinks in my neck and such," I told him.

"Well allow me to help with just that," he purred in my ear.

He pressed against that area of muscle tissue and I tensed up, letting out a small moan as he massaged that area. He then moved downwards, pressing his hands to my buttocks, teasing the flesh that was there. He then moved to my legs, massaging the back of them.

When I felt it press against that area between the thigh and the knee I tensed up, letting out a small cry of both pleasure and surprise, enjoying the feeling of this. I tensed up, watching him smile.

"There you go. You're doing so well," he said to me.

"Thank you," I said, letting out a small moan.

"Now, we can begin tantra," he said to me.

I felt a thrill grow within me as I started to look at him, seeing the way his eyes looked over mine.

The first thing that we must do is connect our breaths," he told me.

To connect our breaths? How does that work?

"How though?"

"We're going to use something called Bliss Breath. First thing you need to do is constrict your throat. Then take a breath in, and you'll hear a sound that's like whispering. Then, you want to exhale and make that sound once more," he explained to me.

I thought he was crazy, but I decided to try it. I took a moment to take a deep breath in, letting my breaths become slow, audible, and easy to use.

"There you go," he replied.

"What's the purpose of this?" I asked.

"It's to help with grounding you. It also will help with a full-body orgasm," he said.

"Full…body?" I said.

Was that even possible? This was something that I'd never heard of.

"Yes, full-body. It's a little different from what you're used to, but just trust me on this," he said.

I did trust him. even though I didn't expect this to feel well…so intimate, it was exciting for me to feel.

"Alright, I'll do that," I said.

"Good. Let's bring our breaths together," Casey said.

We did as he told me, and as we brought the breathing together, I felt that hint of arousal grow within me.

We locked into one another's eyes, and I stared at him.

"You ready?"

"Yes," I breathed out, flushing crimson.

"Alright, lay down on your back," he instructed.

I did as I was told, the robe spilling open and showing my breasts that are exposed for him to see. I looked at him, and he smiled.

"Alright, let's start with a simple breast massage," he said to me.

"Alright."

"Close your eyes," he instructed.

I trusted him. I knew he'd give me pleasure beyond my wildest expectations if he did this. I heard the sound of something being uncapped, and then the sound of something being squirted out. I imagined that it was massage oil, but wasn't sure.

"Alright, let's begin," he said to me.

He rubbed against the very sides of my breast. At first, I didn't really feel much from this. But then his hands moved downwards, the nerves of my body immediately reacting.

"Ahh," I said.

"Don't worry, this is a warmup. It's to help you feel relaxed, and also to help with building arousal," he explained to me.

"A-alright," I told him.

I believed that this would feel better once we continued to explore one another. His hands then moved against the edges of my breasts again, circling the outside. The little, slight touch was enough to make my body react, but then I remembered the breathing. Even though I didn't really see him, the connection that I felt was something different. It was an intimacy that even I didn't expect from this sort of thing.

I jolted slightly, letting out a soft little moan of appreciation and arousal as he continued to do this.

"Very good. Now just relax," he said.

"I'm relaxing as much as I can right now," I said with a laugh.

"I know that you are. But just...watch what happens," he said to me.

He then massaged down towards the ribcage, touching me with the slightest of touches. That was enough to set me on fire, making me suddenly lose my composure. Then, he moved towards the lower abdomen. I felt my body tingle, a rush of pleasure as I responded to his words. His touches also were different too. When it was on the ribcage, it would alternate between lighter touches, and stronger touches, making my body heat up with arousal, need, and something more.

"There we go," he said to me.

He moved his hands upwards, massaging around the areola that I had, teasing my nipples from the outside.

"Ahh," I cried out, feeling them harden against his fingers.

"Don't worry, it's okay for your nipples to get hard. Just relax," he explained to me.

That was definitely a bit easier said than done, but I tried my best to keep my wits about me, relaxing as I felt his hands continue to touch, decorate, and tease against me.

He then encircled his fingers against my nipples, pressing there with the tips of his fingers, and then, lightly pinching them slightly, enjoying the sounds that came out of my mouth.

"Fuck," I said, moving my hips forward.

"There you go, you're feeling good right?" he said.

I felt a feeling of heat as he did this, touching and pinching them lightly, letting his fingers roll against the tips of my nipples. I shivered, moaning.

"Y-yes," I said.

I felt like my body was already on fire, but I knew that this was merely the beginning of it, and I was in for quite the treat.

"Good, if you're ready…we can start with the next part of tantra. The yoni massage?" he asked me.

"What's that?" I asked. I didn't know the terms that were associated with this.

"It's a clitoral massage. And maybe I can teach you other forms of the massage too," he said.

He was such a good teacher that this was already better than I expected. I looked into his eyes, nodding.

"A-alright," I told him.

"There we go. Now sit back and just relax. You can watch my hands and such if you like. Just remember the breathing," he explained.

I'd remember that as best as I could. But my brain was already on edge, and there was definitely a feeling of nervousness that came from this.

He slid his fingers down towards the apex of my legs, but when he stopped near my pussy, his finger extended out. It was merely his pointer finger, but I felt it gently touch the tip of my clitoris.

As I felt that, I let out a small cry of surprise. It was just the tip of his finger! Why did it...feel this good?

"How?" I said.

"Just relax. I'm going to put a little bit of pressure on this. Just take a moment and relax into this," he said.

He started with the slightest of touches, moving from the tip of the clitoris from one side to another, moving from the tiniest of circles to a larger circle against the little nub. The pressure of course started out feather-light, but then became heavier.

I was already a sweating mess. I didn't expect it to feel well...this good.

"Holy shit," I said, the waves of pleasure hitting me hard.

"There we go," he said.

"What are you going to do now?" I asked him.

"Just relax. A bit more teasing. If you're too sensitive for one side, we can tease it," he said.

I knew that the clitoris had a ton of sensations, but I didn't expect this. He then pressed down and started to lightly move the finger against there, then sliding the finger against the edge of my clitoris. He continued to tease the sides, lightly pressing and then pulling on it slightly.

My body was already on edge. He grasped the sides of my clitoris, and then I felt a slight tugging sensation. My eyes widened, my hips moved upwards, and I cried out.

"H-holy shit," I said to him.

I could feel the pleasure, from the tip of my clitoris, all the way down. He then moved his fingers against there, rolling it slightly between the pointer finger, and the index finger, making me suddenly lose control, making me lose my mind, and I couldn't help but feel like I was so close.

But I didn't want to cum yet. This was too good to miss out on, and I loved every single touch this man bestowed onto me. He rolled it around, and my whole body felt the pleasure, surging through every fiber of my body, making me hold the sides of the bench as he did this.

It was then when he slowly tapped his fingers there, making my body respond. A low, guttural scream came from my throat, my whole body on the edge of orgasm. But I didn't feel like this was the end of this for some reason.

"Ahh," I said, feeling the heaviness of the touch, but then, he slowed down.

"Are you ready for more?" he asked me.

"Yes," I breathed out, slowly becoming like putty in this man's hands.

He then spread my lips apart, two fingers slightly curved and entering into me. I felt the fullness of this, but then I felt his hands move against a ridged area.

That set my body on fire. I cried out, feeling his hands lightly press against there, touching slightly.

"There we go. Now, I'm going to stimulate both your clit, but also your g-spot down here. Don't worry, if you orgasm, that's fine," he told me.

I shivered, feeling my body on edge, enjoying the tips of his fingers just barely grazing against there. Then, he slid his fingers forward, and for a moment, I forgot how to speak.

He continued this, his thumb right up against my clit, massaging the area. Making me lose my mind, completely enraptured by the sensation of this. He continued to move his hands there, making me feel the pleasure in every fiber of my being, causing me to hold onto the tip of the massage table, his other hand moving towards my nipples, feeling the sudden force of this making me tense up.

That's when it happened. The waves of pleasure hit me, and my orgasm suddenly made me lose all semblance of control. I cried out, moaning out loud as I continued to feel him do this. It was then when, after a brief second, he then moved his hands towards my nipples, teasing them while also pinching my clit between his thumb, and the feeling of my g-spot being stimulated once more.

This wasn't but one orgasm, nor was it just a series, but it felt like I hit the point of an orgasmic precipice, and I cried out, feeling my hips thrust forward, massaging against the tip of the g-spot, losing my mind, completely enjoying the feeling of this as I continued to feel him tease me, playing with every part of me, my whole being feeling the utter pleasure that came from this.

It was like I was having multiple orgasms, again and again, crying out and thrusting my body forward. I felt the orgasm not just against my pussy, not just from my clit, but from...all over.

The wave of pleasure was one that I enjoyed, one that I could get used to, and something that I couldn't get enough of.

I cried out, pressing my hips forward, losing all semblance of control.

"Holy shit," I screamed out, feeling the last of the orgasmic waves jolt me forward, and I couldn't help but feel like I was not only turned on, but...at peace. It made me feel really good, and then, he pulled his fingers out, teasing them against his lips and licking them.

"Wow," I told him. I didn't know what to say. It was like all of my thought processes were all gone. I never thought that a yoni massage would make me feel this way.

"You good?" he asked.

"Yeah. I'm feeling...amazing really" I told him. It was a form of an orgasm that I never thought I'd get to enjoy.

"This is a really powerful thing. In fact, it's one of the main components. It's a bit different for guys, but it definitely lets you feel that sexual energy that you want to have in your body. And of course, it shows you new sensations," he explained.

"Yeah, I certainly felt some new sensations," I replied.

They were sensations that I didn't really experience up until now.

"Is there...something I can do to you?" I asked him. I didn't want to just have an amazing orgasm and then say fuck it to everything.

"Well, that depends. Do you want to try a massage on me...or do you want to try sex?" he asked me.

I wanted to try both, but honestly, I needed a moment, and I knew that Casey had a pretty fast refractory period.

"Let's...try the massage next. I want to try this with you," I said with a flush.

"There we go. It doesn't have to be something long either. We can take this nice and slow, it's just a matter of connection, and bringing us closer together," he said.

I didn't expect to feel this when I thought of swapping. In truth, I always thought we'd just have sex, but the connection we had was...something more.

That's what I enjoyed about this. I liked the swapping because of how good it normally felt.

"Yes, and we can take this slow, explore the meditative aspects of this, so you can have fun with this too, and learn how to use it," he explained.

"Alright let's try that," I said.

We switched positions, with him in a robe this time.

"Okay, first you want me to lay down, with my legs apart," he said.

"Yeah," I said.

"Good. Now, let's breathe...together," he said.

We both breathed together, an energy and feeling that we felt as we both inhaled and exhaled making me feel a connection.

"Alright, first, I want you to grab the lube, and move it around down there. Don't forget the thighs, the pelvis and pubic bones, testicles, and perineum," he explained to me.

"So, all of those areas?"

"Yeah, just take it slowly. You can move your hands around there, and you should just use your own discretion with this," he said.

I flushed, realizing how he was letting me have this kind of control. I just hoped that I didn't fuck this one up.

"You're sure about this...right?" I said.

"Course I am. I wouldn't be letting you do this if I wasn't," he said.

There was definitely a deeper bond, a sort of trust that was there between both of us as I started to get the lubricant, moving it around there. I put the lubricant into the area, moving my hands first and foremost against the thighs.

I grabbed them, feeling the meaty muscle, with also a little bit of fat on there. I rubbed my hands there, grabbing it hard and softly, and he let out a small hum of approval as I did this, watching me with excitement in his eyes. I continued to watch him relax against my hands, and I did as he said, moving my hands against there, rubbing the edges of his thighs with the smallest of touches.

"There you go...good job," he said, his voice laced with lust and pleasure. I soon felt his hands move towards the sides, relaxing against him.

I then moved my hands upwards towards the pubic bone, lightly resting my hand against there. He reacted to the touch, so I figured a little bit of a massage may be good for him to experience. I started to rub against there, touching, teasing, playing with him as he started to let out a small groan of arousal, of need, and of desire as I continued to press against there, watching his responses.

Then, I moved to the perineum. I flushed realizing that we had this kind of connection there, but I soon moved my hand there, lightly touching it. It didn't take much for him to respond, a small groan of pleasure and need filling the air as I did this. I watched his hands grip the sides as I began to let my fingers stroke there.

Little gentle touches. I also pressed a little bit harder there, watching his eyes widen and his hips move upwards, touching the very edge of my fingers.

"Fuck," he said.

"You good?" I asked.

"Yeah, I just didn't think that this would feel so...good?. I wanted to try this with Melonie, but she thought that it'd be weird," he said.

"Well, she's clearly missing out," I said with a laugh.

I then moved my fingers against there once more, until I could see his cock slowly standing at attention.

"What about your...balls?" I asked, flushing with embarrassment at even asking about this. I didn't expect this to be so intimate, and feel so damn good.

"I want you to massage them. Don't be too rough obviously. But you can pull and fondle them for the most part. If you have fingernails...I can take a little bit of the touch from that, but nothing too crazy," he explained.

This felt way more intimate than I expected, but I took a deep breath, realizing the state of everything, and soon, before I knew it, I moved my hand towards there. At first, I grazed his balls, barely touching them, my face flush with arousal, enjoying the sensation of this. It felt weird touching the soft sacks like this. I thought that they'd be a little bit harder, but they weren't very malleable. I pressed there, slowly pulling on them, massaging them with my fingertips. I took each one in my hands, lightly rubbing my fingers against there, still keeping the same even breath.

He looked at me, his eyes widening as I did this. I didn't really move too hard. I simply just...touched them, teased them against my fingers, watching his body respond to the actions that I took. I continued to lightly fondle them, moving and thumbing over the very tips of his balls. I then moved my fingernails towards the tips of them, grazing there, enjoying the touch from his hands, loving the way that he immediately reacted as I pressed against the edge there.

"Holy fuck," he breathed out.

"Are you good?" I asked him.

"Yeah. Just feels good you know," he said.

"Alright, I'm moving upwards," I said.

I pressed my fingers towards the shaft, slowly moving my touches around. I moved from the base to the tip, using a soft grip at first, then moving the pressure a bit harder, touching against there, watching his eyes widen, and his breathing grow. I started to watch his eyes widen as I started to move my hands in different strokes, starting slowly with a lighter grip, a little faster with a lighter grip, and then harder and slower, feeling his body just become putty in my hands as I continued to move it around.

I then started to twist his cock around in different motions, using one hand at first, then using two, one on top of another as I moved it slowly, and then a little bit quicker in response to this.

I continued to press my hands there, exploring his cock, using different speeds of jerking, of touching, of teasing, and I enjoyed the way he simply let out a series of soft moans, and I couldn't help but feel his body just react.

I continued this for a bit, until I saw the look in his eyes.

I didn't want him to cum yet but he was close.

"Please...down here too," he said.

He lifted his legs up, exposing his prostate. I flushed, realizing what I was about to do.

"Are you sure? It's a little...different for us you know?" I said to him.

"Yes. If you're comfy with it, I'd love for you to do this," he said.

"Alright," I said, flushing crimson at the realization that he wanted me to tease his prostate.

I started to lube up my hands, slowly entering into him. I started to look at him, seeing his body just immediately react.

"Good. You want to...go for the prostate," he said.

"Alright," I said, flushing. I knew where it was. The truth was...Casey let me try different things on him, including femdom, so it didn't seem all that off for me to do this with him in a strange way. That's what I enjoyed about it.

I started to move my fingers inside, finding the little pea-shaped gland that was there, pressing against there. I slowly stimulated it, at first with little touches, and then made them a little bit faster, touching, pressing, teasing the flesh that was there. He let out a series of cries, pressing forward in response to the actions that I took.

And I loved it. I loved seeing him lose control, the slow touch of this making me excited about this. I continued to move my fingers there, doing a similar motion that he did to me down by my own spot.

I continued to massage, stimulating this, and slowly, he gripped the edge of the massage table.

"I'm going to cum," he said.

"Then do so. I know that you can," I told him.

He held the edge of the massage table, giving me a look, and then, he let out a small, low moan as he pushed his hips up, holding onto there, the sound of an orgasm reverberating through the room.

As he finished up, I looked at him, seeing the look of feeling spent, but also, he seemed...happy. I finished up, letting him sit there, taking a moment to process the orgasm that he had.

"Are you.... okay?" I asked.

"Yeah. Amazing," he said.

I flushed, realizing that he probably was in no position to have sex.

"You alright? Do you still...want to try tantric sex?"
I asked him.

"I do. I just...need a moment okay? I'm pretty
amazed at how good this feels," he told me.

I didn't expect it to feel this great if you want the
truth of it. I just thought that it'd feel good, and
would be like a massage, not feeling like the third
eye I had was open, and feeling the slight overtaking
of pleasure as it continued to hold me there.

He left the room, and I sat there, trying to figure out
what to say next. He came back shortly after with
two cups of tea.

"Here. Drink up," he said.

We drank this together, both of us not saying a damn
thing as we looked at one another. He then gave me
a beaming smile.

"That was...amazing really," he said.

"Are you sure though? I don't want to make you
think I overstepped any boundaries and—"

"No, you didn't. I enjoyed the hell out of it. I just
wanted to make sure that you were taken care of too.
The next part involves a connection between two
people. I know we're just swapping, but I feel like we
do have a connection," he explained to me.

I nodded.

"Yeah, I think so too," I told him.

He smiled.

"Yeah, I can tell you feel the same way. The smile on your face. The way you look into my eyes. It's obvious," he added.

I did feel like we were connected. In our own weird way, we were definitely together, enjoying the feelings that we had for one another.

"Do you want to continue then?" I asked.

We finished the tea, and then he nodded.

"Yes, but let's do this at my place. It's a bit more...personal you know?" he said.

He was right. I quickly got dressed, and we took his car over to his place. I didn't know why, but there was something about trying this with him that excited me, that made me happy, and that made me realize that we were definitely learning more about one another as we continued to grow with each other, in a passionate way that we both weren't expecting.

Chapter 3

When we got there, he opened the door, bringing me upstairs. He took some time to light the candles, some incense in the air.

"Melonie hates the smell of this stuff, but I love it," he said.

"It's really not that bad. And it kind of helps set the scene you know?" I said to him.

"It sure does. So how are you feeling after...all of that," he said.

"In truth? Amazing. I feel like I've unlocked something that I didn't expect that I'd love so much," I told him.

I knew that tantric massage was some powerful shit, but I didn't expect this, nor did I expect to do this with someone, building this level of a connection with him. It was weird, I felt more connected with him than I'd felt with Arnold before.

"Alright, so first...we need to get our breathing together, and we can touch," he said.

"Alright," I said.

We slowly undid one another's clothes, breathing in the same way as we did before. The way we breathed was different. We were soon synchronized, touching one another with slow, sensitive strokes.

I moved my hand between his legs, massaging his cock in the same way that I did before. With a slight touch that would make him feel arousal, but nothing too hard. Soon, he was slowly starting to get hard, and I could feel the warm pleasure that came off this start to take over me.

"Are you...good?" he asked me.

"Yes. I'm good," I said, feeling a deep connection, and arousal with him that only made me ache for him more.

"Alright, so we're going to try the yam-yum position. It's based on the energies that involve male and female traits. It doesn't matter though, since we can work on...switching this, and see how it makes you feel," he explained.

"Okay.... what should I do then?" I asked.

I had no idea how this would go, but I was definitely a little bit worried about this too. I felt a little bit embarrassed, but I also wondered what would happen next between us. How could we build this connection even more?

Casey moved over to the pillow that was on the bed, sitting there cross-legged with his cock standing fully at attention.

"Alright, I want you to get on top. You can of course put your legs over my own or you can use a pillow to sit on in my lap. Whatever you want," he told me.

I nodded.

"I think I'm going to sit in your lap," I told him.

I moved towards him, but I didn't insert myself.

"There we go. You need to put your shoulders around me, and we need to be facing one another, touching either at the cheeks, or at the forehead," he said.

"Why is that?" I asked him.

"The energies. Remember the chakras that are a part of this?" he asked.

I didn't spend a bunch of time learning about this, but I did have a vague idea of what he meant.

"Yeah kind of," I said.

"Well, this helps with that sexual energy, moving it between us by going up, and between our bodies," he said.

I nodded. Moving my cheek next to his, feeling our breaths move closely.

"Then, we need to just breathe together," he said.

It was different. Instead of it being focused on massaging, it focused on the two of us bringing our breaths together. We soon synchronized our breaths in the same way that we'd been trying. Then, I started to feel him slowly enter me.

It was very slow at first, but the undulating feeling of his cock inside me made me shiver with delight.

"Holy shit," I said.

"You good? That's our bodies moving together as one. You can take control too. I don't mind letting you do this," he said to me.

"A-alright," I said, feeling a bit embarrassed. He was just letting me take control like this, and I didn't know why, but there was something almost embarrassing about this. But then, I began to dip myself against him, feeling the energy that flowed through me. I arched my body a little bit, feeling the way that it touched and tingled against my body driving me slightly mad.

"Wow," I said, feeling the heat grow through me.

"There you go. Now take it nice and easy. Let's do it together. Take it slow, and find that energy that works together," he said.

I felt his cock move around, slowly moving in circles, holding me a certain way. The connection between us as he did this was different from what I thought. I always thought that it was just sex, but this was something far deeper, more intimate, and more amazing than I expected.

We looked towards one another for a second, feeling our breaths connect as we did this. It tingled within me, making me feel it in every part of my body. From the top of my body over to the bottom of my toes, I could feel the energy, the force, and the connection that was there. The movements were slow, like an undulating wave, but that was perfect for me. It built a deeper pleasure that I thought that I would never get to experience.

He wasn't even getting deep either. But it hit differently. It hit in a way that made me shiver with delight, made me tense up, and made me cry out with complete and utter desire. It felt like I was feeling this all the way from where we connected, all the way up to the top of my body. The way our bodies touched, the connection between us, and the feeling of our bodies as we did this was so nice. It was fun, and it drove me crazy.

We felt our breathing connect, and then, as he pressed in, he touched my nipples, slowly massaging them. The moment he did that changed me. I felt my whole-body tense up, the surge of pleasure roam through me, and that's when I cried out, feeling like all parts of my body had suddenly gotten to the edge of nirvana, feeling the orgasm overtake my whole body, soul, and being.

I cried out, shivering as I looked at him, feeling my entire existence grow, every fiber of my being completely overwhelm me. I then tensed up, crying out, feeling my orgasm match with his, and he groaned.

The way we both orgasmed together was a little bit different from before. I felt a connection on both a spiritual level, and together as two people, two souls with hearts beating as one.

When he pulled away, he looked into my eyes, giving me a soft, subtle kiss, and we stayed there, kissing softly. Then, he pulled back, smiling.

"How was that? Did you enjoy tantra?" he asked me.

"I sure as fuck did. That was...different from what I expected," I said.

I felt like we connected on a physical level, and on a spiritual level, together. It helped fulfill something different. And I don't know, even though we were supposed to just be swapping, a part of me felt conflicted with how good that this felt.

"So, what do you think? Amazing isn't it?"

"Yeah. It's a different feeling. Probably unlike anything I've ever experienced," I told him.

It was a foreign feeling. But there was something exciting about this. He leaned in, grabbing my hand and smiling.

"Good. Because I like seeing you enjoy this. You seem happy. And maybe...we can do this again together," he said.

"Yeah. I want to try and show Arnold this, but I don't think he'll like it that much," I told him.

"Well, it could be our little secret. Maybe you can come over and we can explore tantra together?" he offered.

I didn't think it was necessarily cheating. It was fulfilling a kink, something that felt nice, amazing, and a whole lot different from what I imagined.

"Yeah, I think I could arrange that," I said with a beaming smile.

We got ourselves together and I went to get the car, moving back to where the house was. I saw Melonie leave as soon as I got there, both of us smiling towards one another as we looked into each other's eyes. Even though this wasn't conventional by any means, it was a whole lot of fun.

When I got inside, Arnold was in there, sighing with contentment.

"Hey honey, how did it go?" I asked.

"Pretty good. Did you learn something fun with him?" he asked me.

"Yeah, I did. I'd love to show you it," I told him.

I didn't expect him to immediately smile.

"Sure, I'd love to see what he taught you. Perhaps you can help me...understand tantra as well," he said with a purr.

Even though I didn't think he'd be the biggest fan of this, I wanted to at least see where this would go. The two of us went back to the bedroom, kissing passionately together.

"Okay, so we first and foremost need to synchronize our breathing together. Try to breathe together at the same time," I explained to him.

"But why?" he asked.

"It's to help us connect, build trust and understanding, and to work together. It will benefit both of us," I told him.

He seemed a bit confused by this, but then nodded. We started to try to do this together, and then, when we looked at one another, we started to kiss slowly, breathing as well.

The first time with Arnold was awkward to say the least. He wasn't as into it as I was, and it was hard to truly match the connection. But he did like the touches, that much I was sure of, and I figured if nothing else, he'd enjoy that, and that alone.

While I thought we'd have something a little bit deeper than just an awkward connection, it was fine. I would continue to learn and master tantra with Casey, even if I felt that it would be hard for us to do.

The connection that we shared was something magical, something amazing, and for both of us, with the way that we shared the desire and connection with one another was something amazing, and I knew for a fact that no matter what, that time we share together would be something amazing, something different, and something that we both would be able to enjoy, no matter what.

Just One Night

A Forbidden Desires, Threesome Story

Chapter 1

I looked at Rocky and his girlfriend Celine. Both of them were attractive as hell. They were also way out of my league.

I clutched the textbooks that I had in my hands, seeing them walk by on campus.

"Hey there Marnie," Celine said, waving at me.

I waved back, trying to hide the flush that was there on my face. In truth, I always thought that both Rocky and Celine were attractive.

Rocky of course, was one of my best friends, a guy I'd known since I was in kindergarten. We kept in touch even after we changed schools, and we happened to end up at the same college together. To say that I had a crush on him was a bit of an understatement, given the fact that we still had that same connection after all this time.

But when I found out that Rocky was dating Celine, it made me jealous. When he brought it up to me, I remembered the clenching of my body, the anger that flowed through me, the fact that he did all of this, and it made me feel terrible.

"You're not mad, right? I mean Celine is a wonderful girl, and we're both in the same classes and stuff," he told me.

I didn't want to be mad. I was happy for him, since he finally found a girlfriend that made him happy.

But I couldn't help but feel the jealousy bubbling in my body when he sat down with me, senior year at the school, right before we were going to graduate and go to the same college together.

It sucked even more because I was going to ask him out to prom too, and I felt a bit like a moron as I realized this.

But, there couldn't be anything done. He chose her over me, so I guess I had to just...live with the consequences of this. It pissed me off, but I guess that's just...how it went so to speak.

When I met Celine though, that's when things suddenly changed. Celine was someone who was incredibly familiar, and for a moment, I wondered if I knew her from somewhere. She was pretty, I'll give her that, and I couldn't help but feel like I knew her from somewhere, wherever it might be.

"Who the hell was she?" I asked.

Besides being utterly gorgeous, I didn't know at all. I decided to do a bit of research on this, to see if I could find anything on Celine. I looked her up, trying to figure out who she was.

That's when I realized it.

It was her!

I thought she seemed familiar. But this only made things a little bit more awkward when I realized it. Celine was the daughter of my old babysitter as a kid, a friend that I had for a long time, but then one day, she vanished, along with the babysitter. I tried to ask my parents what happened, but they said that they had to move.

And now, she was dating my best friend.

It felt so wrong, but I felt a bit of jealousy not just for Rocko, but for her too. I realized when I figured it was her that she was definitely the first girl I had a crush on, the first time I had an inkling that I may be bisexual.

The realization made me flush. I mean, how do you explain this one? It made it awkward to say the least, simply because I knew that if I brought this up, shit would be weird between us. But maybe...Rocky would understand?

I don't know for sure. But Rocky seemed to be chill, and Celine seemed to be really nice still too.

When we met up, Celine looked me over, her face curling into that of confusion.

"Something the matter?" I asked. I wondered if she figured it out yet. The secret to who I was. I figured she didn't when she shook her head.

"No. I'm sorry, you just look familiar. Like someone that I knew back in the day, but I can't put a name on it," she said to me.

I didn't know what she meant by any of that, or if it was a good thing.

"Well, I'm happy for Rocky and you," I told her.

"Yeah, I am too. But I'm also glad Rocky has such a good friend like you," she said with a smile on her face.

Those words alone made me flush crimson. I didn't feel like I was a good friend because I had an unbridled crush on him that wouldn't be easily resolved. But maybe...just maybe, one day I'll be able to come forward with it.

About a month had passed since then, and whenever I spent time with Celine, she would look at me, giving me a wry little smile, that little flame of excitement growing within me. I didn't know why, but I felt like...there was something more there.

When we accidentally would brush hands, she'd look at me, red as a tomato. I'd play it off of course, telling her that I was a bit of a space case and forgot. She'd laugh it off too, saying that it was no big deal.

When in reality, it was obvious that the two of us were this close to just losing our cool right then and there. I didn't know why, but I felt like there was something bigger, something going on there, and I couldn't help but feel it grow closer and closer with each passing day.

"Say Marnie? I have a question for you," she said.

"A question about what?" I asked her. Usually, Celine would just make small talk, getting excited about little things until Rocky would show up.

"Oh, it's just...I don't know, you ever just sometimes feel those urges that grow within you that are hard to explain? Things that you want to tell the other person, but you fear what they may say?" she asked.

"Yeah, I get that," I told her.

"I know it's kind of dumb but...I definitely think about that. And I don't know, I feel like you and I knew one another from a long time ago. I wanted to tell Rocky, but he thinks that I'm joking and that I'm imagining things when I say this," she explained to me.

"I don't think you're joking at all," I told her.

"I'm not. But I feel something deeper with you Marnie. Like we had a connection between us that is not known, but it's right there," she said to me.

I didn't know what she was getting at. Maybe it had something to do with what she said, about her knowing me in the past.

Suddenly, before I knew it, her face was right up against mine, her eyes staring at me. Her lips were mere inches away, and she cupped my chin, looking at me.

"Very interesting," she said.

Her lips were so damn close. It took everything within me to bridge the gap, to kiss those lips. But I stopped myself.

I knew that if I did this, it would ruin things with Rocky. But ugh, just one kiss. That's all I wanted. I wasn't asking for some sort of large-scale thing. I just wanted to know what her lips on mine felt like.

She then smiled.

"It's all good. I'm sorry if I'm being weird. I just feel a deep connection with you. Maybe.... I don't know, it's stupid but I almost feel like kissing you would help. But I couldn't do that to Rocky. I feel like...if I do that, it will break his trust. He's already a little jealous of me and you, you know," Celine said.

I looked at Celine, taking in and drinking her beautiful face up. The long, flowy red hair, the blue eyes, her tall, thin frame with a bit of curve. She was beautiful, something I couldn't help but marvel at. And in truth, I felt like she was the pretty one, and I was just the goblin that tagged along with them.

"Yeah, I figured," I told her, feeling a bit disappointed that I couldn't kiss her.

"But maybe...down the road something can change. You never know what may happen," she pointed out.

I wanted to ask her about this, but then, before I knew it, she was gone, leaving me alone. I sat there, mulling on what the hell had just happened.

What did this mean for us? What could happen now? I had no fucking clue, and I felt like I was being tricked or something. Maybe this was all a figment of my imagination though, and he really didn't feel anything towards me, and neither did she.

I guess that settles it. I guess. I'll just…. see what will happens now.

I packed my bags and went to class, trying to figure out the cryptic meaning behind Celine's words, but still at a loss for what that meant.

Chapter 2

About three months had passed since that weird confession Celine gave to me, and they stuck together strongly. I was jealous about that. If I could have either of them for just one night, I'd be happy as a clam.

When I was alone in my own room at the dorms, I'd sit there, my hands down my pants, touching myself, teasing my clit with one finger, touching my right nipple with my other hand. I let out a series of small breaths, imagining both Celine and Rocky taking me.

First, I imagined Rocky. I wondered how good his cock felt, how big he was, or even how he'd taste. I wondered what it'd feel like if he took my virginity, if he finished within me, all of that. I wondered what would happen if this happened one time, and the future that this would mean for us.

But then my thoughts would shift to Celine. The feeling of her soft lips against my own, her hands against my breasts, touching the fingertips of my hands, moving her own fingertips down to my nipples, painting little touches against the edges, teasing the very tips with the pads of her fingers, causing little moans to come out of me.

Then I imagined her between my legs, eating me out, making me feel good. That alone was usually enough for me to orgasm, the tiniest, smallest of moans coming out of me.

"Celine...."

There was suddenly a knock at the door. I let out a small squeak as I quickly got dressed, hoping that it wasn't my roommate, or worse, Celine who would hear her name from my lips and wonder what the hell was going on.

I quickly made my way over to the doorway, opening it, coming face-to-face with Rocky, who was looking at me with a concerned glance.

"There you are. I didn't hear you come out right away, was a little bit worried for a second," he said.

"Sorry, I was getting ready," I lied. It was such a shit lie, but it had to be enough for him to believe it.

"Anyways, I wanted to talk to you about something. Is it cool if I come in?" he asked me.

I shrugged.

"Be my guest. I don't have classes for a little bit," I admitted.

I just hoped that it didn't smell like I had just masturbated in there. He then opened the door, closing it, sitting at the desk that I had. He paused, trying to figure out what to do, or even what to say.

"What's the matter?" I inquired.

"It's about Celine," he said to me.

"What about her?"

"I don't know, but she talks about you a lot. She keeps telling me how nice you are, how sweet. Your name gets brought up a lot by her, and whenever I look at her...I notice that she's got this little look of excitement on her face. I don't get it. Does she...like you? Have you done anything with her?" he asked me.

I shook my head.

"No. but I can see it too kind of. She seems very passionate about me. I don't want to make you feel bad or anything but—"

"No, it's not that at all Marnie! In fact, I'm sorry, I know that this is a bit embarrassing, but the truth is...I definitely wanted to see if there was something that...I don't know you could do about this," he asked me.

"What do you mean?"

He pursed his lips, trying to find the correct words for this. I could tell he was flustered, when he spoke.

"It's just...I don't know, I feel like...fuck this is embarrassing," he admitted.

"It doesn't have to be though. You can tell me Rocky—"

"Can we have a threesome? With you," he spat out, turning red as a tomato. Now it was my turn to feel a bit flabbergasted.

"With, you mean like...both of you with me?" I asked him.

He nodded.

"Yes. I'm sorry, this is embarrassing. I wanted to ask you if you wanted this. I know that it's probably rude, considering you're like...not with anyone and we're together, but I think it'd be good for her and all," he admitted, turning red in response.

I looked at him, trying to figure out what to say. This was definitely a bit different from what I thought would happen.

"Are you sure about this? I don't want you to find it weird or anything," I told him.

"Not at all! In fact, I think it'd be quite nice. Just the three of us," he offered to me.

I mean, this was what I thought about. I quickly nodded.

"Yeah, I could do that. But only if she's cool with it," I told him.

"She'd be very cool with it. And I know that you like me Marnie. That much is obvious. I figured...it could help her get it out of her system, and we could get to the bottom of this. And I know that you'd like that., I'm sure that one night together might be...just what you're looking for," he told me.

I thought about that. One night together. That was exciting, and while I did feel a flush of embarrassment as he said those words, I liked the sound of it.

"Sure. I'd love that," I told him.

"Oh, thank fuck you're not weirded out. I felt bad for kind of just admitting this to you like that, but I'm glad that you're cool with it," he said.

I flushed.

"Yeah, I've liked you. And the truth is…I remembered Celine. She was a girl I had a crush on. I wanted both of you, but I knew that it was wrong, especially since you were together and all," I said.

"Well, just for one night, you can tag along, and be included. Why don't you come over to my place this Friday? Not the dorm obviously, but you know, my house," he said.

"What about your mom?" I asked him.

"She'll be out, along with my dad. They left the house to Celine and I, but I'm sure a third would be a fun little thing for both of us," he told me with a wink.

I blushed, but nodded.

"Sure," I said to him.

He left the room, and I pursed my lips, thinking about this. He was my best friend, and Celine was an old friend. I didn't think I'd get a chance like this like…ever. But there was something about this that excited me, that made me feel like…deep down this would all work itself out, and things would soon be more different than I ever imagined. I guess I'd better get ready for Friday.

The excitement and desire that I felt in my body was only growing even more so, and there was definitely that feeling of lust, of need, and of excitement that came with the fact that one of the deepest, darkest secrets that I had was about to be fulfilled, and I'd be at the receiving end of it all.

Chapter 3

Friday couldn't come soon enough. I got my homework done a little bit earlier so that I didn't have to worry about this, but that didn't stop the excitement that I felt in my heart at the prospect of this.

When Friday rolled around, he told me seven would be the best time. At seven on the dot, I pulled up, and when I got there, Celine was at the front of the doorway, waving.

"There you are," she said.

"Hey," I replied. Did she know what was going to happen?

"Come on in," she said.

We walked inside, and things all seemed very...simple at this point. I looked at her, and then she motioned upstairs.

"By the way Rocky is up there. He told me to bring you up," she told me.

"Sure," I said.

We got up there, and Rocky seemed to be smiling.

"There you are," he said.

"Hey," I said to him.

"I was thinking we could play a little game first," he said.

What kind of game did he have planned? I flushed at this, realizing what was going on. I didn't know what would happen next, but then he got out a bottle.

"Spin the bottle," he said.

That sly ass bastard. He was totally planning this so he could get Celine to admit her feelings, but then he stopped.

"Or we could do truth or dare," he said.

"Let's try the latter," Celine said.

"Yeah," I replied.

We started playing, and soon, things seemed to be pretty normal. At first, it was a bit nerve-wracking, since I didn't know if he'd bring up some sort of dare between Celine and I but then, at the one-time Celine picked truth, Rocky spoke with a smile on his face.

"Alright Celine, this is for you, and for Marnie," he began.

"Sure," she said to us.

"Did you know Marnie before I got together with you?" he said to her.

She paused, flushing, and then, she nodded.

"Yeah. I didn't know if it was true or not. I thought that I was seeing things, but then, when we met up, I realized this wasn't just my brain fucking with me.

You really were the girl that my mom babysat when I was younger," she said.

My eyes widened in surprise.

"You remembered that?" I asked her.

"Yeah, I did," she said with a beaming grin.

"Good," I told her with a small smile.

"Alright...your turn," Rocky said to Celine.

"I guess this one is for you then Marnie," she said.

"What do you mean?" I asked her.

"Truth or dare?" she asked me.

"Umm...truth?" I asked her. I felt my heart race as I said those words. Did I make the right choice?

Her lips curled into that of a smile. I think I started something.

"Did you ever have a crush on me back when we were younger?" she asked me.

I paused, feeling the embarrassment flush against my face.

"You mean like a...crush crush?" I asked her.

"Yeah, like you liked me," she teased, giving me a small grin.

Fuck this was embarrassing. I felt nervous, unsure about it, but I certainly was a little bit scared by this. I then started to look at her, feeling the excitement and worry cross my face.

"Alright fine, I guess I can tell you," I told her.

She looked at me, unsure of what was going to happen next.

"Well come on, spill," she said.

I felt the nervousness take over my body, feeling like I was about to make a mistake uttering these words. When I finally said it.

"Yeah, I had a big crush on you back then. I wanted to tell you, but I didn't know for sure. We were also kind of young and all," I said.

"Aww that's cute," she purred in my ear.

I immediately reddened, feeling a bit embarrassed by it all.

"Well...now what?" I asked them.

"It's your turn," Rocky said, a grin on his face.

"Fine. What about you Celine? Did you ever have a crush on me?" I asked her.

I realized this was supposed to be truth or dare, but I spat it out. I didn't even care at this point. She flushed, but then nodded.

"Yeah," she said.

I realized she felt the same way that I did. There was something almost...exciting about this, and it made me feel good about this.

"Alright then. Truth or dare Marnie," Rocky said.

"Umm...dare?" I asked him.

"I dare you to kiss Celine," he said, giving me a small, devilish smile on his face. I felt the sudden realization of what was about to happen hit me.

She liked me and well...I liked her. I knew that after tonight we wouldn't be able to explore this, but there was something almost fun about this.

I moved closer, feeling my heart skip a beat. I didn't know why, but there was something exciting about this. I wanted to know exactly what would transpire next. Then, our lips were right up against one another, the closeness of our breaths obvious, the realization that she was right there, kissable and within range, and that of course made me feel a rush of excitement.

"Are you...sure about this?" I asked her.

"Damn sure," she said to me with a surefire smile on her face.

Here goes nothing. I leaned in, pressing my lips to hers. We kissed for a second, and for a moment, I got lost in her lips, realizing how soft, sensual, and amazing they felt. I kissed her passionately, enjoying the feeling of this as the two of us simply just stayed there, enjoying the feeling of this.

For a long time, we simply just sat there, making out, enjoying the sensation of it all. We continued to touch, tease, and make out. She pressed her tongue to my own, and our tongues moved and mingled. We made out for what felt like forever, but was probably just a few minutes. I heard the sound of a throat being cleared, and then, I felt her pull back, looking at Rocky with a smile on her face.

"What's the matter Rocky? Jealous?" She asked him.

"Little bit. You two just look so fucking hot," he said, his voice filled with a haze of lust.

"Well, maybe we should take this over to the bed, so we can both explore and tease you appropriately," Celine said.

I realized that I was under her control, and I enjoyed every single moment of this.

"Yeah, I'd love that," I said.

She giggled, touching me, and then bringing me over to the bed. I felt Rocky move behind me, sharing a kiss with Celine before she moved back over to my lips, touching the tip of them and looking at me.

"Is this what you've wanted? Your best friend and your childhood crush to be here, taking care of you? Making you the star of the show tonight? Because that's the intent that I have with you," she purred.

Just hearing those words coming out her mouth was just so damn arousing. That's what turned me on when it came to this. I enjoyed the fact that she was just so nice to me, and how she teased me with just the utterance of a couple of words.

She moved her hands against my chin and neck, plunging downwards and touching my curves. I felt a pair of hands on my waist, and then I was turned back. Soon, my lips were against Rocky's.

His lips were a bit harder, and it surprised me at how good this felt. We kissed passionately together, enjoying the feeling of one another, the excitement and need only making me hunger for more from him. He continued to make out with me, our tongues touching, teasing, enjoying the sensation of one another.

He was a good kisser, a whole lot better than I thought, and I felt his hands move upwards, cupping my breasts through the confines of my clothing. I let out a small gasp, enjoying the touch of this.

"My you've grown Marnie," Rocky said in my ear, touching my breasts, feeling them up, and then letting his hands dance against my nipples.

"Not fair. I want to touch them too," Celine said.

"You'll get your chance babe. I want to tease them a little bit first," he said to me.

I flushed, feeling his hands move against my nipples, playing with them against the very tips of his fingers. I suddenly felt my whole body relax, immediately melting into his touch, loving every single moment of this.

I continued to feel like this was only driving me madder and madder. He knew exactly how to touch me, and then, I felt Celine's soft lips against my own, giving me deep kisses, and then peppering ones that went down my body, teasing my neck with the softest of touches.

In truth, I felt like I was in heaven, enjoying the feeling of two amazing people, just completely immersed in making me feel amazing, completely in awe at the sensation of what this meant for me, and completely enraptured in the feelings of pleasure that escaped from my mouth, enjoying the feeling of this too.

Suddenly, she got towards my collarbone, kissing the tip of it, and then sucking on the flesh there. She hit a spot that made me tense up, moaning out loud and in pleasure as I felt my hips arch, and my body suddenly change into that of complete lust, arousal, and pleasure as well.

She continued to tease me for a little bit, enjoying the sounds that I made, when I felt my sweater get pulled over my head. A pair of hands was on my back, no doubt Rocky's, and when he touched me there, I let out a small gasp of pleasure and arousal, enjoying the feeling of his hands there, touching, teasing, and making me feel amazing. He then moved to the back of my bra, undoing the clasp, and Celine quickly pawed it off, making me blush.

My breasts were out there, on full display for her. She moved her hands slightly, grasping them and touching them.

"So soft. They're bigger than mine too. I'm a little jealous," she said.

Rocky grabbed one of my breasts, teasing the tips of them with little touches and grazes.

"I'll be damned. They are," he told me.

I shivered, moaning slightly as I felt them both continue to touch my breasts. Rocky's touches were both against the nipple and I felt him grope and tease the breast itself.

He teased my nipples, causing me to let out a small cry, tensing up and moaning slightly as I felt the pleasure grow within me. This felt amazing, and he knew exactly how to tease me.

But that didn't compare to what Celine had in store for more. She moved towards my other breast, touching the very tip of it with her lips, looking at me with a wry smile.

"Look at you. You have the cutest breasts, and you make adorable sounds. I can't get enough of this," she purred.

I shivered, feeling the slightest bit of arousal as I began to watch her move towards the tip of my nipple. She breathed on it, smiling as she saw me squirm around.

"Look at you. All turned on. How cute," she said.

"Only because you keep doing this to me," I said with a flush.

"And I'll do so much more honey," she said.

I wanted her to do this. Especially since it... well...it felt really good. She moved towards the tip of my nipple, just over it, and she gave it a tentative lick.

That, combined with the little pinching that came from Rocky, was enough to make my head roll back, the pleasure seeped through me. I shivered, enjoying the little touch of her lips. It was the smallest of licks and little nips at my breasts, but that alone was enough to drive me crazy, turning me on, making me enjoy everything.

She smiled, moving towards the tip, touching the edge with her tongue, flicking it there. She then wrapped her lips around it, encircling against the nipple, watching my eyes widen in amazement as she began to suckle on it slowly but surely, holding my breasts there as she touched them. I let out a small hum, but then I let out another small little cry, enjoying the feeling of her hands against them, and Rocky's hands touching my nipples too.

The sensation of all of this was enough to drive me crazy, and I felt like I was moments away from losing it right then and there. I wanted more, my body and mind craving so much more from this. It made me hungry for them, aching for both of them, and it made me realize just how much I desired it all.

Then, that's when I felt Rocky move away from me. Celine pushed me down into the bed, smiling at me as she hovered over my body, touching the sides, letting her fingers skate over my breasts, lightly teasing, pinching, and playing with them as I looked at her.

"What's the matter? Enjoying this?" she said to me.

"Y-yes," I told her.

Realizing just how turned on I was by the mere mention of her voice. She teased my nipples, enjoying the sounds of pleasure that came out of my mouth. It was clear that she was enjoying this as much as I was, if not more for some reason. I guess there was the fact that she was of course, able to finally get what she wanted.

Which of course was to turn me on, make me feel good, and pleasure me like no other.

She then continued to press her fingers against the edge of my nipples, touching, teasing, playing with them for a little bit before letting her hands settle on downwards. She then got to where my skirt was, sliding that off of me. I shivered as she moved her hands against my thighs, touching them, squeezing them, the little touches of her hands against my thighs turning me on.

"Fuck," I said.

"Someone's a bit excited, aren't we?" she teased.

"Damn right...I am," I told her.

I was at a loss for words. I had no idea what else to say other than the fact that I was massively turned on and aroused by the fact that she was teasing me like this, making me the woman of her dreams, turning me on and enjoying every single aspect of this.

She continued to let her hands slither on upwards, until of course, she got between my legs. She cupped the heat there, making me shiver with delight, lightly gasping in surprise as I felt her hands right up against there, looking me in the eyes with smiles on her face.

She pressed against the heat, touching there slightly, the little touches were enough to make me shiver with delight, I let out a series of small gasps, and moved my hips slightly.

"Look at you. So turned on already," she purred, pressing her fingers against me.

"Please," I said, feeling my whole body at its limit. I needed them. I wanted her to touch me. I wanted to feel her against me.

She smiled, moving her hands towards the sides of my hips, pressing against there, looking at me and licking her lips. She slowly started to move my panties off, pushing them off to the side, looking at me with a grin on her face.

"There we go. That's better," she purred.

She moved her hands, exploring towards me, pressing against my folds. I let out a small cry, surprised by how good her hands felt. They were soft, sensual, and seductive. She looked me in the eyes, licking her lips as she pressed a finger into me.

"Ahh!" I cried out.

"Is this your first time?" she asked me.

I whimpered, nodding in response.

"Yes," I told her.

"Good. I'll take it nice and slow then," she said.

She began to press her fingers there, in and out, touching me and teasing me slightly. She then moved forward, touching the tip of my clit with her tongue, licking around, pressing against there.

I shivered, moaning out loud as I felt her lips and hands completely overtake me. This felt amazing, too fucking good, and I was losing all semblance of control right then and there. I looked over at Rocky, who was smiling.

"While she gets you ready, why don't I give you a taste," he said.

I realized what he meant. He undid his pants, pulling them down, tossing them along with the boxers off to the side. His large cock sprang out, and my eyes widened in surprise at this.

"Woah," I said, looking at the size of that thing. It was big, and the fact that he was going to put that inside of me both made me nervous, but also made me excited.

I leaned forward, licking the tip, and I felt the tongue that was right near my clit lick at the same time as well. I started to explore this, feeling him groan against me.

"Don't worry, it won't bite," he said with a laugh.

I knew that it wouldn't bite. I started to move my lips against his cock, bringing them down the length of it. And as I did that, another finger slipped into me, pressing in and out, teasing me.

I shivered. It both felt different, but also felt right as I felt these two just completely overtake me, making me enjoy the sensation of this far more than I cared to admit. I realized that they were enjoying this as much as I was, and it was then when, after a few more thrusts, I felt her fingers curl up slightly, hitting one spot, and as she did that, my hips bucked, and my pussy tightened. I then moved my lips against the very base of his cock, feeling it there, and he groaned, holding my head there as he fucked my throat. I suddenly felt completely aroused, turned on, and needing more from this man, completely excited about it all, and craving more.

I suddenly felt his cock thrust in and out of me, making me shiver with delight, enjoying the sensation of all of this. I craved more of this, desired so much more, and as I continued to move against there, thrusting in and out, suddenly feeling my whole-body tense up, I could feel the fingers curl up inside of me, breach me, and making my hips move against her, moaning around his cock.

"Fuck I'm already feeling it," he said.

He pulled me off of him, sitting down, sheathing his cock with a condom. He looked at me with an expectant glance, and in truth, I felt the excitement and desire that grew over me come to light.

I wanted this. I wanted him, and I wanted her as well. I slowly moved against him, feeling my whole body become tense with a bit of nervousness. Would this feel good? Or was I going to regret it.

I looked over at her, and then, moments later she smiled.

"There we go," she said to me.

I started to slide down on it, at first feeling a little bit nervous, but then, as it breached me, I let out a small groan of pain, and discomfort as well, only to suddenly feel him fill me the hell up.

"Fuck," I cried out, feeling like my whole body was on edge, completely amazed by how this felt. He held me there, looking at me.

"You good?" he said.

"Yeah," I told him.

I began to move and rock, only to see Celine move herself, pulling off her own clothes. I saw her small lithe body, but what interested me more was her wet pussy. I reached out, touching her there, slipping a finger in, my lips kissing the tips of her folds, my tongue reaching out and teasing her.

"There you go. Good job," she cooed into my ear.

There was something nice about hearing that praise that sent me to a whole new world. I quickly began to lick with excitement, looking at her as she smiled at me, holding my head there.

While she did that, I felt Rocky adjust the position, so that I was on my hands and knees, and soon, he began to thrust.

When he did that, I suddenly cried out around her, eating her out while also moaning into her muff. She held my head there, letting out a small cry.

"Yes. Good girl," she told me.

She held me there, and I felt his thrusts move deeper and deeper, making me shiver with delight, enjoying everything that was happening as well. As I started to feel him thrust deeper and deeper, and even faster as well, I licked that one spot on her, causing her to tense up, let out a small moan, holding me there as she thrust hard.

I stuck another finger in, pressing upwards, watching her tense, cry out, holding me there as she came against my face.

After a few more thrusts, I felt another hand move forward, pressing against my clit, holding it there as I started shivering. Everything was driving me crazy. I was already on the edge from this alone. After a few more thrusts, I began to tense up, holding onto the bed as I came hard, feeling my own desire drip out of me.

This was so good, but then, Rocky pulled out, motioning for Celine to come over. He quickly slipped it into her, fucking her hard.

Celine pushed me down again, going to town on my pussy, holding the tip of my clit, teasing it, letting her tongue snake out and move against there. I let out a series of small moans, completely enthralled. After a few brief moments, I saw Rocky's hands move down, rubbing against her.

"Fuck babe! I'm so close," she said.

"I am too. Want me to spray your faces," he said.

Celine looked at me, and I nodded.

"Yeah," she said.

He pulled out, tossing the condom to the side, and Celine grabbed me so that I was right in front of her, sitting there with her as we looked at him. I watched as Rocky jerked his cock, looking at me with a smile on his face.

"For both of you," he said.

That's when he released. His cum sprayed our faces, and I quickly licked it up. It tasted a whole hell of a lot better than I thought, and Celine savored the taste of it, smiling.

"There we go," she said.

He finished up, sitting back down and laying on the bed.

I quickly cleaned off my face, and Celine did the same thing. We didn't say a word to one another after all of that, completely amazed by how good this was, and how he made both of us feel.

In truth, for the first time, this shit felt really good. Even though I was in a little bit of pain because of what had happened.

We all sat on the bed together, none of us saying a damn thing for a bit. I mean, what would we say at this point? What do you say after you have sex with your best friend and his girlfriend who you had a crush on a long time ago?

"Well, that was great," Rocky finally said, breaking the awkward silence that was there.

"Well, it was more than just great Rocky. I had a wonderful time. And it did...help with a fantasy of mine," Celine said.

I looked to Celine, smiling.

"Same here. I'll be the first to admit that this is exactly what I wanted," I told them.

"Indeed. It was a lot of fun. And you're pretty cute," she replied with a smirk.

I flushed, feeling a little bit of embarrassment as I said those things. I turned to Rocky, feeling bad about this.

"I'm sorry for never telling you how I felt. I always...thought it was wrong to admit how I felt," I told him. I mean, I'd been harboring a stupid crush for a long time, but maybe he understood that.

"It's okay. I understand that Marnie. And in truth, I always thought you were kind of cute too, but I never wanted to date. It would impact the friendship that we already had. I didn't want that," he said.

It was kind of a silly reason to not want this, but I guess that's just the way that he did things.

"Well regardless, I'm just happy about what has happened," I told them.

"Indeed. If you want, you can stick around with us tonight. We were just going to chill once we were done with you," Celine said.

"Yeah. And don't think we don't want to include you Marnie. In fact, I think you awoke us to something that I didn't expect to enjoy," he told me.

I flushed, realizing that they did the same as well.

"You know, it's kind of the same way. And for someone to take my virginity, I'm sure as fuck glad it was both of you," I admitted.

I know that sounded pretty fucking stupid. I mean, I don't know if they felt the same way. But Rocky laughed, pushing his brown hair back, his blue eyes looking into my own.

"Well, I'm glad that I could make you happy Marnie," he said.

I pushed my black hair back, smiling at him.

"Yeah, I'm glad that we could do this too," I replied.

We spent the rest of the evening hanging out, having a good time together. The two of us did feel like our friendship was a little different now, and Celine was a part of our lives too.

But in truth, I didn't mind it. I was happy that I could have these two here with me, in my life, and they gave me a first time that I could enjoy. Even though I was short, thick with big breasts, and awkward, I felt like I really got to experience this with them, in a way that made me smile.